Nobody Told Me What I Need to Know

Nobody
Told Me What
I Need to Know

HILA COLMAN

WILLIAM MORROW AND COMPANY
NEW YORK   1984

Printed in the United States of America.

10 9 8 7 6 5 4 3 2 1

DESIGN BY CINDY SIMON

Library of Congress Cataloging in Publication Data
Colman, Hila.   Nobody told me what I need to know.
   Summary: A cultured, protected teenager longs to break out of her confined
life through her friendship with a very different boy.
   I. Title.   PZ7.C7Nm   1984   [Fic]   84-8673
ISBN 0-688-03869-7

FOR JOEL

One

WE WATCHED THE HOUSE ACROSS THE street go up as if we were kids at the circus or had paid a fortune for tickets to a show. My dad, mom, and I giggled about it a lot. Every evening we'd look out our front windows and stare at what the workmen had done that day.

Whatever they did, one of us would think it was terrible. "Good grief," my father said at one point. "They're putting phony stucco on the front. How can people do that to a house? It wouldn't be so bad if they'd only leave it alone."

"It's a hideous house no matter what they do to it," my mother said. "Thank goodness our house is set back and we have our trees. But I'm going to put in a row of hemlocks so we don't have to see it." The new house was pretty peculiar—the fake Spanish just didn't belong on a country road in the Catskill Mountains of New York.

We all three looked down on the O'Carneys before we ever laid eyes on them. Our family, you see, was special. I was brought up to believe that from the minute I was born. I am Alix Angell, my father is Edward Angell, and my mother is Constance Angell, and don't dare call her Connie or her husband Eddie. My grandfather was a successful businessman, but my father was not the least bit interested in the manufacture of plumbing fixtures. He turned up his nose at going into his father's business. Instead, he chose to be a sculptor. A very good sculptor, but since he looked down on anything commercial (he was an "artist," you see) he never made a lot of money. He met my mother, a weaver, at a craft show; they got married, and here I am.

We're not poor, but we don't live like other people do. In fact, in all my fifteen years, I can't remember us ever being ordinary middle-class people. My mother inherited what my father calls "old money," so we are able to have a rather beautiful Victorian house built in 1850—complete with turrets and a tower, big rooms with high ceilings, old plumbing, and poor insulation—you get the picture? We live on the outskirts of the village of Mill Pond in the foothills of the Catskills. My parents had bought a lot of land, so we have tremendous woods and a hill behind the house, as well as a barn that has been made into a studio for my father. My father drives a car that's ten years old and my mother refuses to own a dishwasher, but we have a fantastic stereo and tapes of every symphony and opera ever written—no television set, of course—books galore, a few fabulous antiques, and original oil paintings. Every afternoon my parents drink tea out of china cups that belonged to my great-grandmother.

When the O'Carneys moved in about a month after their house was finished, we found out that they were just the opposite. We watched the moving men unload massive overstuffed chairs and sofas, ugly chests of drawers, and vinyl tables. My mother laughed when a tremendous artificial tree was taken out of the truck, followed by fake house plants. "Can you imagine, artificial plants in the country?"

The O'Carneys themselves arrived in a huge white Cadillac accompanied by a motorboat on a trailer, a motorcycle, and about every mechanical device you ever heard of: power mower, snow-blower, electric saws. You name it, they had it.

"Maybe they plan to build a high rise," my father said caustically. "They'll blow the power out if they turn all that stuff on."

We had only glimpses of the O'Carneys themselves, usually when they were standing outside their garage obviously discussing how and where to house all their paraphernalia. We couldn't hear what they were saying but it was funny to watch their elaborate gestures. Mrs. O'Carney seemed pretty in a doll-like way. Very petite, with lots of blond hair. Mr. O'Carney was a large, rugged-looking man, clean-shaven and handsome in a way that indicated he knew it. I could tell, without hearing him, that he was telling everyone what to do. Everyone was mainly their son, who looked like he was around seventeen, and a daughter about eleven or twelve. The boy was almost as tall as his father, with the same strong nose and chin, but softer looking, not so aggressively male, and much slimmer. Very good-looking, too. The daughter didn't look like anyone else in the family. She had dark, wavy hair, was very slim and a little exotic.

Mill Pond was such a nothing village in New York State—great skiing country, but too far from

New York City to commute—that it seemed the last place in the world for a family like the O'Carneys. What were they doing here?

We had our formal introduction to them on the Saturday after they moved in. It was the middle of the afternoon, the time when my parents listened to the radio broadcast of an opera. I heard the thump of our brass knocker on the front door, but since everyone we know comes in the side door near the garden, I couldn't imagine who it could be.

When I opened the door, I was surprised to see Mr. O'Carney standing there with a huge bunch of lilacs in his hand.

"Hello. I'm Joe O'Carney, your new neighbor. Just wanted to stop by to say hello." He thrust the lilacs into my hand. "Are your parents home?" He had stepped inside and obviously could hear the music. He was even better looking close up, with bright, dark eyes, bushy eyebrows, and gray in his thick hair that made him look important.

I took the flowers and wondered how he could miss seeing the huge lilac bushes we had along the side of our house. But I thought it was nice of him anyway.

"Mom, Dad," I called. "Mr. O'Carney is here."

My parents appeared, and I was sure that my

mother was annoyed at being interrupted.

"Hi." Mr. O'Carney put out his hand to my father and nodded to my mother.

"Thought neighbors should be friendly," he said jovially. "We're new around here and we don't know many people." He gave a wide smile. "Actually we don't know a soul. Just wanted to say hello. How about stopping over for a drink later? Mrs. O'Carney is out shopping, or she'd have come with me. She's sure glad to have a woman neighbor close by." He winked at my father. "You know women, they talk on the phone half the morning and then see each other twenty minutes later for lunch."

"I'm afraid that would leave me out," my mother said, not very gracious. "I work most of the day."

If Mr. O'Carney was embarrassed by my mother's put-down, he didn't show it. "Well, we'll be around. If you want to come over later, just drop in. Bar's open at five o'clock," he added with a grin.

"Thank you, maybe some other time," my father said. "And thank you for the flowers. We were glad your builder didn't cut those bushes down. We enjoy the lilacs every spring."

"Oh, yes, yes, we're glad to have them." He looked a little confused and left quickly.

My mother sighed when the door closed behind him. "I hope that is the beginning and the end of our friendship with the O'Carneys. I can just see myself spending the morning talking on the telephone to her." She laughed.

"You weren't very cordial to him," I said. "It was nice of him to come over."

"Alix darling, if you encourage someone like that, there'd be no stopping him. It's better to get things straight right from the beginning. We don't want to be friends with the O'Carneys."

"I know that. But you don't have to be so—" I stopped. I was going to say "snotty" but I thought better of it.

My mother, who can sometimes read my mind at the most inconvenient times, gave me a sharp look.

My next encounter with an O'Carney was on Monday morning, while I was waiting for the school bus. The girl came out of her house and joined me. When I saw her close up, I decided she was younger than I had thought. Maybe not even ten. Her gypsy looks were spoiled by a sulky expression on her face.

"I'm not supposed to be going to school," she announced to me without a "Hi" or "Good morning." "They told me I wouldn't have to start until the fall."

"Who's they?" I asked, not that I cared.

"My parents, of course." She looked at me as though I might be demented. She tossed her head. "But I got a new bike. Ten speeds. A Peugeot—that's French. My father has an Alfa Romeo. That's Italian."

"So what?"

"So nothing. What kind of a car does your father drive?"

"My father rides a horse," I said.

The dope took me seriously. "What kind? I had a Palamino when we lived in California. Real neat. I hated coming here."

"Why did you?"

"My father's business. He's building some houses here. Park Grove. We move to wherever he's building. He thinks he's going to make a fortune. He always says that, but my mother says he never will. She says he gets all excited but he never watches the bottom line. I don't know what the bottom line is, do you?" She was so candid about her family's personal affairs that I was embarrassed—but dying for her to tell me more.

"I'm not sure. I think the bottom line tells you if you're going to make money or not."

But she was off to something else. "I wish my father was a gangster, then he'd be rich. I'm going to marry the head of the mob when I grow up."

"You'll probably get killed," I said cheerfully.

Then our bus came, so that was the end of our conversation. She didn't sit with me. I watched her look around and then go and sit next to David Bloom, the best-looking boy in our school. She introduced herself—her name was Eileen, I overheard her say—and immediately began talking to him a mile a minute.

Since it was getting near final exams, I didn't think much about the O'Carneys for the next several days. Except when I heard their son's motorcycle. Then I'd run to the window and watch him zooming in or out of their driveway. When I saw him coming out, I watched him until he disappeared down the road and wondered where he was going. He made me feel aware that I was missing something.

Until recently, my life had always been uncomplicated. Although I went to parties, played softball, and went for hikes in the woods with other kids from school, I had never gotten tied up with any one group. My parents hated group activities and were very selective about their friends. Occasionally, they and some other couple went out to dinner or to a movie. They liked to take me with them a lot of the time, and since none of their friends had children my age, I was used to spending almost as much time with grownups as with kids. It had been rather fun. Julie, my only close friend, thought it would be boring, but I liked to listen to them talk, and I got a lot of attention.

But ever since I turned fifteen, I had felt a change. It wasn't something that happened overnight; I didn't wake up one morning and feel that everything was different. Rather, small things occurred that made me aware of how the kids at school saw me, which made me stop and think. Like one day at lunch in the cafeteria I was sitting with Julie, Liz Myers, and Tony Ransome. I didn't know Liz or Tony well, so I just listened as the three of them talked about going to a rock concert.

"Would you like to come?" Liz asked me.

Julie answered for me. "Oh, Alix doesn't listen to rock. She's too highbrow for that," she said good-naturedly.

"That's her loss," Liz said, but she looked at me as if I were a strange animal. "You *never* listen? You don't have *any* rock records?" She said it as if I'd told her I never cleaned my teeth. "I'd die without mine." The subject was dropped, but Liz and Tony kind of skirted around me after that, making me feel I was a one-of-a-kind museum piece to be looked at but not touched.

There were other things, too. Like not being invited to some parties. I screwed up my courage one evening at Julie's house and asked her about that.

"You going to Patti Wayne's party Saturday night?" I asked casually.

Julie, who is no dope, gave me a sharp look. "Yes, I am."

"I wasn't invited," I said.

"I know." She looked uncomfortable. "It's not your kind of party."

"What do you mean by that?"

"You wouldn't like it. It's all couples. And— well, they pair off and make out."

"Oh." I didn't look at her but at some books on her desk. "I know what you mean. You all think I'm kind of weird, don't you?"

"I don't," she said quickly. "But, well, everyone's growing up, and things are different. They're not kid parties anymore."

"And I'm still a kid?" I looked at her.

"In some ways. But you are different, your family is different. There's nothing wrong with the way you are, but I guess Patti thought that you wouldn't fit in. And you wouldn't. You know yourself you wouldn't. You have to just be yourself, Alix. I think you're terrific. Your parents are terrific, too; they're special. You're all special."

"I don't want to be special," I burst out. "All my life I've been told we're special. Who needs it? It stinks."

Julie was shocked by the emotion in my voice. I surprised myself. "But you're interesting," she said. "You know about things I don't. I'd never even read Emily Dickinson until you gave me her book of poems. You know more about good music, you've been to museums. I've never been inside the Metropolitan Museum of Art, and you've been there dozens of times. I think you're very lucky."

"Would you like to be like me?" I asked her, looking straight into her eyes.

She looked away. "I couldn't be," she said after a few minutes. "I'm me, and you're you."

"You wouldn't like it. You know you wouldn't." I turned away. "I don't want to be like me either." That was the end of our conversation.

I suppose one of the things that attracted me to the O'Carney boy was my growing desire to be like other kids. He, and his family, were the opposite of everything my family valued. It was we, not they, who were different from other people, and I was beginning to find out how out of touch my family was with the rest of the world.

Besides, he was so darn attractive. Of course I knew other boys, had gone out on a few dates, and received a couple of good-night kisses; but none of it was exciting, not at all the way Julie explained it was for her—like riding a roller coaster, she said. Yet whenever I saw him, I felt so alive. It was a strange feeling that I'd never had before. And it was silly, since there was nothing that I knew about him that should have given me that funny little quiver, as if my destiny had arrived and was waiting for me. In fact, I didn't even know his name. And I agreed with Mom and Dad that his parents' house was awful, and his family was vulgar.

But all the same, I thought of him constantly. I thought about how cute he was, and how he always looked as if he were totally absorbed in something. And when he raced in and out on his bike, he was so exciting.

I wanted to meet him, to get to know him. I wanted him to notice me. I wanted to be part of that excitement, to find out what the quivers meant. I'd never been on a roller coaster, and I wanted to find out what it was like.

Two

"PROBABLY," JULIE SAID TO ME, "WHEN YOU meet him he will turn out to be the world's biggest creep." We were walking into the village after school to celebrate the last day of exams, but we couldn't think of anything more exciting to do than eat hot-fudge sundaes.

"I'm sure he will be," I said unenthusiastically. I'd been telling myself that right along. How could he not be with that family, especially that sister of his? I had made it a point not to come out for the bus in the morning until the last minute so I wouldn't have to listen to her talk: how much her new sweater and skirt cost, her new designer jeans, the gigantic birthday party she'd had in California just before she came east. It was all disgusting. Yet I was dying to meet her brother.

I finally did meet him—in the laundromat, of all places. Our washing machine was out of order, and the repairman hadn't come to fix it yet. There was a dry cleaning place attached to the laundromat, and he came in to pick up some clothes while I was washing our two loads. I looked a mess. It was Saturday morning, and I'd gone out in a hurry because my father was anxious to leave. He was dropping me off on his way to a local gallery that was exhibiting a few small pieces of his sculpture. I hadn't washed my hair—I'd hardly brushed it—and I had on my oldest jeans and shirt because I was going to clean up my room when I got home.

He looked terrific. He had on a beautiful blue shirt the color of his eyes, immaculate white jeans, and expensive-looking sandals. I wanted to die, half-hoping he wouldn't recognize me. I think for a minute he didn't, and then his face broke into a wide, kind of amused smile.

"Hi," he said. "You're my neighbor, aren't you?"

"Yes, I am," I said brilliantly.

He held out his hand. "I'm Nick O'Carney."

"I'm Alix Angell." We shook hands solemnly.

"Alix Angell. That's a pretty name. Are you an angel?" His smile changed his face, made him look better than just handsome.

"No, far from it. Do you like angels?"

"No. Devils are more my kind."

We both noticed as the two machines in front of me stopped. "Are they yours?" he asked.

"Yes. I guess I'd better empty them. People are waiting."

"You want a ride home?"

"On your motorcycle?" I asked foolishly.

"No, I've got the car."

"I have to dry the clothes," I said dubiously.

"Will that take long?"

"About twenty minutes to half an hour. You'd better not wait, but thanks a lot."

"I have a few errands to do in the village. I'll come back."

He didn't give me a chance to say yes or no but picked up his clothes on their hangers and left. I was glad I didn't have a chance to tell him that I had a ride home with my father. I was to call him when I was finished. I put our clothes in the dryers, ran to the public phone, and gave the gallery a message for my father that he didn't have to pick me up.

Then I sat down to catch my breath. Nick was nothing like what I had imagined. He wasn't at all uppity, but warm and friendly. And he certainly wasn't a creep. He made me feel quivery and comfortable at the same time. I know that sounds impossible, but it's true. I don't know how it can be that your heart can go thump, thump, and at the same time feel immediately at home with a person, but that's how it was for me with Nick O'Carney, right from the start.

I was just taking the clothes out of the dryers when he came back. He carried the basket out to the car, and we both stopped and looked at the car, then at each other. He had his father's sports car, just room for two, and there was no place in the world for that large clothes basket.

"You could carry it on your head," Nick said.

"Like native women? No thanks. I think I can hold it in my lap."

Nick looked dubious. "It's bigger than you are. It's bigger than both of us," he added with his incredible smile. "Well, here goes nothing."

He held the basket while I climbed into the car, then handed it to me. Just my luck—to be sitting in a fantastic Alfa Romeo sports car, looking a mess with a huge clothes basket on my lap.

"Do you like living here?" I asked after he'd started the car.

He shrugged. "I don't much care where I live. One place isn't much different from another."

"I'd hate to move. I love my house. Don't you miss yours?"

"No, we've moved around so much, I'm used to it."

"That must be awful, moving all the time."

"Why?" He seemed genuinely surprised. "Staying in the same place can be worse."

"If you hated the place it would. But don't you get attached to anything? To a house, a neighborhood, people? I was born in our house, it means something to me. I love our hillside, I love the woods, the stream that runs through our property and then under the road to yours. I know every tree, every wildflower that comes up—it means a lot. I suppose if you move around a house is just a house."

"You bet it is. I guess I'm attached to different things. My motorcycle—that's power, that's something. If this car was mine, I'd be attached to that. They can do something—get me from one place to another—and they're beautiful pieces of machinery besides. A house—well, it's just a lot of wood or stone or bricks."

"Oh, no. A house has a personality, character. It's like the people living in it. You can tell a lot about people just looking at their houses," I said unthinkingly.

He laughed. "Then you should be decrepit and old, looking at your house. It needs a coat of paint," he added. "You don't." He gave me a sidelong look.

"We never paint our house. We like it to look

weather-beaten. Besides, that wasn't what I meant," I said. "People don't look like their houses, but you can tell what kind of people live in certain houses."

"Forget it," he said, and I realized he was bored with the conversation.

When he stopped in our driveway he said, "Can I call you up sometime? Go to a movie or something?"

"Sure, if you'd like to."

"I'd like to."

He helped me out with the basket and then zoomed into his own drive.

I felt absolutely confused. I told myself that he was shallow and materialistic, that he had no taste and could probably talk about nothing but cars and motorcycles. But my heart was thumping at the thought that he'd call me. He was so friendly and so handsome.

Of course my mother saw him bring me home. "What were you doing with that boy?" she asked in her quiet voice.

"He gave me a lift from the laundromat. He was really nice, he came back to get me after the clothes were dry."

"Be careful, darling. I'm sure he's not the kind of boy you'll want to be friends with."

"I don't know. I'll have to see."

My mother opened her eyes wide. "But, Alix, his family is so vulgar. They're not our kind."

Our eyes met. Then my mother, in her lovely way, smiled and her eyes crinkled up. "I sound awful, don't I? 'Not our kind,' " she said, mocking herself. "What a thing to say! But you do know what I mean, don't you? Just do be careful."

"I will," I said, aware, perhaps for the first time, that behind my mother's gentleness was a strong, stubborn will, not unlike my own.

Despite the air of confidence I put on in front of my mother, I wasn't sure of Nick at all. I couldn't think of a good reason why he should want me. Of course, he didn't know anyone else, but that wasn't much of a reason and wouldn't last long, anyway. After I finished cleaning up my room that Saturday, I took a shower, washed my hair, put on clean jeans, and examined my reflection in the mirror.

I didn't know what to make of myself. If someone wanted to rate me from one to ten, where would I stand? As I stared at the slender, brown-eyed girl with the shoulder-length, honey-colored hair who stared back at me from the mirror, I tried to sort out my thoughts: Mom and Dad thought I was pretty, even beautiful, but what parents think doesn't count. Julie's admired my legs, and a boy in school once said it was too bad that a pretty girl like me was stuck-up. I knew I wasn't stuck-up at all. Anything but. Yet everyone I knew was a million times more interesting than I was. I was dull, and I didn't know any of the things other girls talk about. So how could Nick O'Carney possibly be interested in me?

That was that. I turned away from my reflection and wondered if and when he would call me.

Three

I CAN'T EXACTLY SAY THAT NICK O'CARNEY rushed to the telephone. He took his time about calling me. I went from the depths of agonizing despair to giving up and recklessly going to Stockbridge with my parents to see a new play—although I was positive I would then miss Nick's call.

A week after we'd met, he telephoned late one afternoon. It had been the longest week in the history of the world.

"What're you doing?" he asked.

"Nothing much."

"Want to go for a ride?"

"Sure."

"Be outside in five minutes." Big, macho, authoritative. Okay, I was willing to be swept off my feet. Ride into the sunset in an Alfa Romeo. Why not?

I was outside in exactly five minutes and so was he. I had had just enough time to brush my hair and leave a note for my parents, who were out walking.

Nick leaned over and opened the car door for me. "You get to use your father's car a lot," I remarked.

"Yeah. He's over looking at the property, and he's got a company car he uses for business. I luck out."

"Where are we going?"

"No place in particular. Except, is there any open field around here, away from houses?"

"What for?"

"You'll see when we get there." He'd been driving slowly along our road.

"There's a dirt road not far from here that ends up in some open fields. It's not a great road for a car. Sometimes it gets flooded out."

"I'll try it. You get floods around here?"

"There was a big one five years ago. You think our stream is so quiet and gentle, you should have seen it then. It was wild. You know how it runs behind my father's studio? Well some of his pieces got ruined. It just missed getting into our house. We had no road, we couldn't drive in or out for days. It was a mess."

"It must have been fun."

"It wasn't any fun, believe me. A woman who lived where our stream meets the river drowned."

"She should have gotten out."

I turned to look at him. He was serious. "How can you be so callous about someone's life?" I said curtly. What was I doing with this jerk anyway?

But then he turned around and said innocently, "That was a dumb thing to say, wasn't it?"

That was Nick, I was discovering. Coming out with some inane observation and then mocking himself. It was hard to know when to take him seriously.

We drove along to the dirt road and Nick didn't seem to care that it was muddy. I was worried about getting stuck, but I didn't say anything. Getting stuck with him might be very nice. But Nick managed to keep the car going; when the road petered out, he pulled over to the side and we got out. As I had told him, the road ended in some open fields, with a hill on the other side. The fields were beautiful, covered with mustard plants that looked golden in the fading sun. The sky was turning pink and yellow, producing that magical, special light you get on a spring evening before dark.

"It's perfect," Nick said.

"It's beautiful."

"I don't care about that, it's just right for what I wanted." I should have known he wasn't admiring the mustard field.

"What do you want?"

"You'll see." He took a bundle wrapped in paper out of the car and started to walk toward the hill. He walked quickly, and I had trouble keeping up with him. There was no path, so we had to make our way through the underbrush.

"What are you going to do?" I was getting annoyed with his silence.

"You'll see," he said. "Be patient."

"Maybe I won't like it."

He didn't answer but kept on going. We climbed to the top of the hill, and I was beginning to feel foolish. The sun had almost set, the light was changing every minute, and it was going to be dark in a short time.

"I think we should go back," I said. "It's going to be dark, and we won't find our way."

"I thought you were a country girl," Nick said. "You can't get lost in an open field. We're not in the woods."

"We won't know what direction the car is. It's a big field."

"Don't worry. I didn't expect you to be scared. Anyway, this place is perfect." He stopped at a clearing, where it looked as if someone had once had an open fire. "Made to order."

He squatted down and opened the bundle he'd been carrying. To my surprise he took out an assortment of fireworks. I was stunned.

"Where'd you get those?" I asked, astonished.

"I have ways."

"Aren't they illegal?"

"I don't know. Are they?" he asked carelessly.

"Is that what you came here for?"

"Sure. It'll be fun. I love fireworks. We'll have a private celebration."

I must have looked dubious, because he said, "What's the matter?"

"I don't know. It just seems crazy."

"I like doing crazy things."

"Do you always do things like this?"

He cleared away a space for the fireworks before he answered. Sitting down outside the circle he'd made, he said, "I'm going to wait till it gets darker." Then he turned to me. "Yeah, I guess I do do crazy things. Why not?"

I sat down on a rock near him. I didn't answer his question. Instead, I asked him another one.

"What kind of things?" I was very curious.

He gave his sideways, lovable grin. "I was thrown out of school. That's why I'm not going till the fall, that is, if anyone'll take me."

"You mean you were expelled? What for?" It was exciting sitting up on the hill in the fading sunlight with him. There were soft bird and animal sounds around us. I was fascinated.

"Oh, just for a party. In someone's house."

"You wouldn't get expelled just for a party. What'd you do?"

He sat there grinning at me. "W-e-l-l . . . " He stretched it out like it was two words. "You see, the house was empty. Nobody'd been in it for years. It was just there. We didn't even have to break in, one window was broken. So we went in and had a party. A friend and I were the ones who got caught. The police drove up, but the others got out before they came. We didn't hurt anything. They said we broke the window, so they got us for breaking and entering. Dumb cops."

I looked at him in awe. "Did you go to jail?"

"Naw. We were put on probation. But we got kicked out of school. There were a couple of other things, too," he said carelessly.

"What kind of things?"

"Hey, what's going on? You look like you never heard of kids getting into trouble. Don't the kids around here have any fun? Doesn't anyone in this hick town go drag-racing, or skinny-dipping, or have pot parties even?"

"Is all that fun?"

"Sure it is. You don't know anything. I bet you never smoked pot or drank gin or did anything. You don't know what it's all about."

I had to admit that I had never done any of those things. Nor had any of my friends. I knew some kids in school got into trouble, but I always assumed they were from broken homes or had other family problems. As my mother would say, they weren't our kind. "I didn't know kids like you would break the law. I mean, kids from good homes and nice parents . . . " I stopped, embarrassed.

"There's a lot you don't know. Where've you been all your life? Some of the kids I went around with were rich. Their fathers had big jobs and they lived in fantastic houses. That doesn't make any difference. Poor kids went around with us, too. My best friend's father hadn't had a job in two years. Hal, he's a terrific guy, I miss him like the devil. He had an old Chevy he'd remade that could beat any car on the road; and boy, when it came to beer, he could outdrink anyone."

"Where'd he get the money if his father wasn't working?"

"He'd pick up a job whenever he could. He was a great mechanic, and he'd get jobs fixing people's cars. He was a good guy."

It was getting really dark, and I told Nick I thought we should get the fireworks going. He set a few out carefully, and I thought again, watching him, how different he was from anyone I'd ever known and how terribly exciting. He'd done things that the other boys wouldn't even dream of doing. It made me feel wonderfully wicked, closer to other kids in school, to know that my parents would disapprove of him thoroughly—much more than they even did before—if they knew all these things about him.

Swish . . . boom . . . one rocket after another zoomed through the air and burst into showers of stars. After lighting each one, Nick stepped back and stood beside me, his hand on my shoulder. I felt so alive; I'd never done anything so outrageous before, especially nothing illegal.

"Did you hate moving away from your friends?" I asked him between bursts.

He looked surprised. "I miss Hal, but that's all. I told you before—we move so much it doesn't matter."

Since he didn't seem to want to talk about this, I didn't ask any more questions. I didn't want him to think I was prying, although I was very curious about him and his whole family. They all seemed so out of place here as if they had made a mistake and gotten off at the wrong station.

When the last firecracker went off I was sad. I didn't want the evening to come to an end, and for the first time in my life I didn't want to go home. I dreaded the soft-spoken, quiet sameness of our house, the low music, my parents' conversations about the books they were reading. Suddenly I hated the image of my mother tiptoeing around my father when he sat, as he often did, staring into the fire, as if he were some fantastic master with great and special thoughts who must not be disturbed. Or the way he held out his arm for her when they went into dinner. I used to want to be part of their tableaux, their gracefulness, and even sometimes felt hurt and excluded by the way they looked at each other and not at me. But thinking about them now I thought, how silly they are, they're always playacting. They're not real.

I was so deep in thought that I was taken by surprise when Nick bent over and kissed me lightly on the mouth. He smelled smoky and woodsy. I didn't know what he expected me to do next, but I didn't have to worry. He took me by the hand and we walked together down the hill and found our way back to his car.

While we drove home I kept thinking about his

kiss and what it meant. Was it the beginning of something? Was he testing me out to see what I'd do?

"Don't you miss your girl?" I asked him.

"What girl?" he asked, surprised.

"Your girl in California." I was embarrassed and sorry I'd started the conversation.

Nick laughed. "You're a funny kid. I had a lot of girls. You have a lot to learn. How old are you anyway?"

"I'll be sixteen," I said. I didn't know how to lie.

"I'll be eighteen in about six months, but I'm about thirty-five compared to you."

"I'm sorry," I said foolishly.

He put out his hand and patted my knee. "That's all right, you'll grow up. You're pretty, do you know that?"

"Not really. But I'm glad. Thank you for saying so."

"You're welcome." Then he laughed again. "You really are funny."

Just as I expected, when I got home there was a Mozart sonata on the stereo and my parents were each having a glass of sherry. Since the evening had turned cool, they were sitting in front of the fire. My mother had on a long Mexican skirt and gold, antique earrings, and my father wore brown corduroys and a blue sweater over a blue shirt. They both had their legs stretched out toward the fire, my mother on the sofa and my father in a deep armchair. They are both tall and slim, and good-looking in a pale, refined way. Actually, they look alike, with smooth, fine dark hair, which my mother pulls back into a knot and my father wears a little long and shaggy. They have similiar long, thin noses, although my mother has dark eyes and my father's are blue.

"Where've you been, darling?" My mother stretched out an arm to me and motioned me to sit beside her.

But I stood uncertainly between the two of them. The only light was from the fire and from one lamp, which threw a shaft of light and shadows through the open arch from the dining room. I could see that the table was set for dinner.

"I was out with Nick O'Carney," I said bluntly.

"You were?" My mother sounded only mildly surprised. "We heard shots, and we thought it was he, shooting."

"They weren't shots. It was fireworks. I didn't think you could hear them down here."

"Fireworks?" My father lifted his head enough to look at me. "What on earth for?"

"Just for fun. They were neat."

"Oh, really?" my father said. "What's so 'neat' about fireworks? Sounds childish to me."

"What can you and that boy possibly have to talk about?" my mother said in a tone that was cross for her.

"We have lots to talk about," I said glibly. "Loads."

My parents exchanged glances, and I felt that I could see into their minds: He's a bad influence, and his effect is starting already. We shall have to discuss it.

"What's for dinner?"

"Trout amandine and a spinach soufflé," my mother said.

"Why don't we ever have hot dogs or hamburgers, the way other people do? Or a pizza? Let's go out for a pizza," I said rashly. "We can eat the other stuff another night." After feeling so free with Nick, I needed to get out of the house. I felt that I was being smothered or was fading into the walls, that I was going to melt into a shadow and never remember what Nick's kiss had felt like.

My parents were very calm. "Oh, pizza." My mother turned up her nose and gave a light laugh. "After the lovely meal I've cooked you want *pizza?*"

My father said, "McDonald's next, I suppose. Plastic food. You'll have to do better than that, sweetheart, if you want to get these two bodies away from this lovely fire and delicious dinner." Then he stood up and offered an arm each to my mother and me. "May I?" he said with mock exaggeration and led us to the dining room.

My heart was thumping and my blood boiling. Their calm dismissal made me want to scream, to have a temper tantrum, but I felt unable to open my mouth. I sat down at the candlelit table with them and waited till my mother put the soufflé into the oven, then dutifully ate the mushroom soup she brought in from the kitchen.

It's too late, I thought dismally, desperately. I'm glued in here, and I'll never get unstuck.

After dinner I went up to my room wanting to do something violent. But I didn't know what to do. That was the most depressing thought of all, that I didn't even know how to express a strong feeling of anger. Like our house—like them—I was a nonperson, a body with no blood in my veins.

Four

I TOLD JULIE ABOUT NICK AND THE FIRECRACK-
ers, about everything except the kiss. I knew
she would think I was silly for taking one kiss
seriously, but she didn't know how little experience I'd had. When I read Jane Austen I felt more
like those girls than my contemporaries, a real dud
in today's world.

Julie said, "Forget about him. He sounds like a
nut. He doesn't seem right for you."

"He's not right for me, that's what I like," I
said. "I don't want a boy who's just like me. What
would be the sense? I can learn a lot from Nick."

Julie gave me a dubious look. "You might learn
all the wrong things. You shouldn't try to be like
everyone else. You're being different is what makes
you so special."

"A fat lot of good that does me. Everyone else is having a good time while I sit home and listen to my parents' music. I'll never meet anyone—I'll be a grumpy, frustrated old lady." I was close to tears.

Julie was sympathetic, but her words only made me feel more doomed than ever. "No, you'll marry an artist or a college professor and have genius children. You'll be an artist or a writer yourself, and you'll have a beautiful, serene life while the rest of us are fighting our way through the rat race."

"I don't want a dull, serene life," I said fiercely. "I want drama, turmoil."

"Be an actress," Julie said sensibly. She was suddenly proud of the idea. "That's exactly right for you, I don't know why we never thought of it before."

"Because," I said dismally, "I'm neither beautiful nor talented."

"You're not conventionally pretty, but you have an actress's face—all your emotions show, and your face is always changing. And how do you know you're not talented?"

I didn't answer. I figured she was just trying to cheer me up.

I didn't see Nick for several days and decided

he had found out how dull and backward I was. The next word from the O'Carneys was an invitation for the three of us to come to a party the following Saturday night. It came in the form of a short note on violet monogrammed paper from Dyan O'Carney.

At dinner that night my parents discussed how to gracefully get out of it. "Couldn't we say we have out-of-town guests coming?" my mother suggested.

"They'll see there's no one here. Or they'll say to bring them." My father cut into a large shrimp and chewed it carefully.

"Why can't we go? I think it would be rude not to," I said. "They *are* neighbors."

"That's just it. If we go, we'll have to ask them back, and there'll be no end to it. I don't want to get involved with them." My mother looked stubborn.

"You don't want to get involved with anyone or anything," I said crossly. "You two just want to sit here cut off from the rest of the world. You don't even care what's going on. The whole world could blow up, and you'd still be sitting here making your sculpture and weaving your cloth."

My father looked amused. "That might be a good thing. That's what people did way back in the early beginnings of civilization, and it might not hurt to start all over again." Then, more seriously, he looked at me and said, "What makes you so eager to befriend the O'Carneys? Is it that boy Nick?"

"I don't think it's nice not to be friendly. You two make such a thing about the quality of life, that everything in a house should be well designed—Mama will search out a beautiful kettle instead of just something to boil water in—and yet you can be rude to perfectly good people. It seems hypocritical to me."

"That's a strong word," my father said.

"We're not rude, and we don't know whether they're good or not," my mother said. "I would say we're being consistent. As you said, we are picky, and we don't like everything. From what we've seen so far, we think they're uninteresting and crude, products of a mass-minded culture."

"But that's just the point. How can you really know what they're like? You've only talked with Mr. O'Carney for a few seconds and never even met Mrs. O'Carney. You haven't given them a chance. For all you know they might be fascinating." Of course I didn't believe that, and as Julie said, everything shows on my face; so they laughed, and then so did I. "But it isn't funny," I said. "I think we should go. If it's awful, you don't have to ask them back."

My parents looked at each other. Then my father said, "All right, if you really want to go, we shall. But this doesn't mean that we want to become friends with them or that we want to encourage any friendship between you and that boy. We are going just to be decent neighbors."

"I understand," I said briefly.

My father changed the subject by telling my mother about some new psychological theory he'd just been reading about. But I couldn't stop thinking about what they had just said. I was so mixed up. I loved my parents, but I was realizing more and more that they were snobs. They had good taste and were different from ordinary people, but they were too aware of it. It was as if they were always seeing themselves in a mirror and making sure that the reflection matched their own image of who and what they were. I was starting to wish that sometimes things would be out of place, that the pictures would be crooked and there'd be coffee spilled on the rug, or that they'd yell at each other. I wondered what it would be like to live on a street where parents screamed at their children for doing something wrong, where kids played ball and had fights, and men came home smelling of beer. After feeling so alive with Nick the night of the fireworks, I now felt stifled in our rarified existence.

My father had said the O'Carneys were very materialistic, that all they cared about were their possessions and making money. Yet I didn't see that that was so terrible—my father celebrated when he sold a piece of his sculpture, and my mother made me take the antique quilt off my bed before I sat on it. She cared about her possessions. They shouldn't be so critical of others, because they weren't perfect, either.

My mother is really peculiar. Saturday night she insisted that I wear a skirt and a good blouse to the O'Carneys'. After all the fuss she made about not wanting to go, she then wanted everyone to be dressed properly.

"But Eileen will be wearing jeans, and Mrs. O'Carney will probably be in pants. She never wears skirts," I told my mother.

"There's no reason we should accommodate to their standards."

So we went across the road looking elegant, my mother in a long cotton skirt and gold earrings, my father wearing a turtleneck under a handsome jacket, and me feeling foolish in my skirt and blouse. Naturally, the O'Carneys were all in designer jeans.

It was the first time we'd been in their house,

and while I had secretly prayed it would be pretty, I had to admit it was awful. There was too much furniture, and none of it belonged in a country house: satin sofas next to ultramodern vinyl tables, silk lampshades over cutesy lamps. It was a jumble that might not have been so bad if half the stuff was taken out. I was afraid to look at my mother out of fear that she would make me laugh.

Worst of all, the room was dominated by a huge television set with a video game attachment which everyone concentrated on. They all turned around for a moment and nodded as we came in, and Mrs. O'Carney introduced us to Mr. O'Carney's parents. Only Nick's father came forward to shake my father's hand. Space was made for us in front of the television, and we watched Nick unsuccessfully try to get Space Invaders killed off. And as soon as one game was finished, one of them would start playing another one. While a game was on, no one talked except for exclamations about it. Mr. O'Carney consumed a lot of liquor, and he kept insisting—with little success—that my father join him.

I felt terribly embarrassed, but it was as much for my parents as for the O'Carneys. Mrs. O'Carney wasn't as intrigued with the video games as the rest of her family, and she flitted about bringing in plates of potato chips and snacks that disappeared rapidly in the vicinity of Nick and Eileen. She also kept beseeching my mother to have a drink and finally persuaded her to take a glass of white wine. I felt sorry for her. I had the feeling that she was eager to impress Mr. O'Carney's parents with her cultured neighbors.

Her elegant neighbors, however, were not helping. My mother could barely conceal her uneasy boredom, and my father's attempts at conversation with Mr. O'Carney or his parents failed dismally.

I thought the evening might pick up when Mr. O'Carney's partner, a small, round, mild-mannered man, arrived, but he sat down, lit a cigar, and discussed the stock market with Nick's grandfather.

At ten-thirty Mrs. O'Carney brought out a plate of sandwiches, a huge chocolate cake, and coffee. Not knowing what else to do, I had been watching the games with Nick, Eileen, and Mr. O'Carney. But Nick had hardly paid any attention to me, and I was getting to feel more and more like an extra limb. The food looked good, so I went over and sat next to my mother.

Mrs. O'Carney sat down on the other side of my mother. "I am so happy for Nick," she said, "to have Alix next door. A lovely girl like Alix is just what he needs. She can do so much for him." She had lowered her voice and bent closer to my mother, but I heard every word she said. Each new sentence made me freeze with a terrible sense that I was watching someone dig my grave. "Nick is a good boy, but he is easily influenced by the wrong people, and it will be just wonderful for him to have an intelligent, cultured girl like Alix as a friend." She smiled across my mother at me. "Perhaps more than just an ordinary friend," she said meaningfully.

My mother was speechless. She just kind of sputtered and took a big sip of her coffee. I was horrified. If anything in the world was going to turn Nick against me, it would be his mother pushing him and telling him I was "a good influence." That was the last thing in the world Nick O'Carney wanted in a girlfriend. And that was the last thing in the world I wanted to be. Here I was dying to be wicked, to do wild things, to make Nick pay attention to me, and I was being presented as "an intelligent, cultured girl." In other words a drag, a creep, a dull wallflower.

The last straw was when she handed me two tickets to a chamber music concert to be held in the chapel of a private prep school in town. Fortunately, my mother had gone to the bathroom, so she wasn't there. "Someone in the village sold these to me," Mrs. O'Carney said with a bright smile. "It's a benefit for a scholarship fund, I believe. I thought it would be nice if you invited Nick to go with you. Don't tell him the tickets came from me," she added in a wicked whisper. "I'm sure it's just the kind of thing you would enjoy, and it'll be wonderful for Nick."

Not knowing what else to do, I accepted the tickets she put in my hand. I murmured a thank you and put them in my pocket before my mother came back.

Nick left the television set to get some food, and I saw him talking earnestly to my father. I wondered what on earth those two could be saying to each other. After they finished their conversation, Nick came over to me and rather awkwardly got me up from between our mothers. We sat in a bay window and tried to talk. I suspected that he felt as uncomfortable as I did, sensing that both mothers were covertly watching us. What he didn't know and I did, however, was the great difference in their points of view: his mother wanting us to get close and my mother having a fit at the possibility. The whole thing was so ludicrous I was tempted to tell him, but was afraid that he'd tell his mother what I said, and I couldn't do that to her.

"Family parties are the worst drag," Nick said. "And this one is worse than most. Thank God for Space Invaders."

"We're not family," I said.

"My mother always thinks of close neighbors as one big happy family," Nick said in a way that made me suspect she had gone through all these motions before in the various places where they had lived. I felt sorry for her.

It was with tremendous relief that I saw my mother get up and announce that it was time for us to go home. My father agreed promptly, and had no trouble disengaging himself from the other men, who were discussing the merits and short-comings of food and service on various airlines.

We thanked the O'Carneys properly and went outside to the wonderful fresh smell of the spring night. No one spoke, but my mother breathed an audible sigh of relief. Then my father said softly, "We did our duty, and never again."

Five,

I WAS HEARTSICK. THIS COULD ONLY HAPPEN TO me: Here I was longing for Nick to be a bad influence on me, and I was asked to be a good influence on him. What could be more perverse?

Sunday afternoon after the O'Carneys' "party," Nick came over. When I saw him standing at our front door, so well dressed and super-looking, I was speechless, and secretly pleased, because I thought he had come over to see me. But then he asked to see my father. Apparently, when he and Dad were talking last night, Nick asked to visit his studio. He'd never seen a sculptor at work and he was curious. Oh, well, I consoled myself, at least my father seems to like him enough to show him around his inner sanctum.

The crazy thing was, though, that up until then I had wanted my parents to like him. But when he came in and shook hands with my father, I had a sinking feeling that if my father took a shine to him, I'd be the loser. I wanted Nick for myself, my secret, wicked passion—someone completely outside of my parents' uppity world. I wished we hadn't gone to the O'Carneys' stupid nonparty.

My father took Nick to the studio and motioned that I should come, too. We followed my father through to the back of the house and out to the red converted barn. I loved the studio. It was one huge room about two stories high, with an open, cathedral ceiling supported by heavy oak beams. The back wall opposite the wide doors was solid stone, broken by a fireplace; but the other two walls had long, narrow windows, and there were two skylights. My father liked to work in wood, and the place smelled of the various kinds he used. There were half-finished clay pieces around as well as some finished stone figures.

Nick was impressed. His face showed a mixture of awe and admiration as he looked around the room and then ambled about examining my father's work. Naturally my father was pleased; he was such a funny mixture—half of him never wanted to part with a piece and the other half wanted to show off what he did. But his face gave him away as he beamed at Nick. "That's Alix when she was eight years old," he said as Nick stopped to study a small figure in stone of a child's head and nude torso.

Nick looked at me and then at the figure. He grinned. "That's neat, that's real neat. Say, that'll be around a hundred years from now, after you're dead. Probably be worth a lot of money, wouldn't it?"

"That's a cheerful thought," I said. "Is that all you have to say, that it'll be worth money? What about what it looks like? It happens to be very beautiful." Sometimes, I had to admit, Nick's materialism did annoy me. Besides, that piece was my favorite. I hoped my father would never sell it, and I think he felt the same way. A couple of people had wanted to buy it, but he had turned them down.

"Oh, sure, it's nice. But you know," he said, turning to my father, "couldn't you make dozens, hundreds of these? Then you could keep this one and sell the others. I bet you'd make a fortune."

My father looked at him in astonishment. I wasn't sure whether he'd throw him out of the studio or laugh. He did neither. He answered him quite seriously. "I wouldn't make anything. This would be worth nothing if I made hundreds. A work of art is valuable because it is unique, because it was fashioned by an artist. Reproductions are manufactured, they are not the same. Now, mind you, sometimes there are good reproductions and people enjoy having them, but still they are not works of art."

"I don't get the difference. If they look the same, I don't understand what's wrong."

"No, I guess you wouldn't understand, and it's hard to explain. Anyway an original and a reproduction don't look the same. Now if you two will go along I may get some work done."

"Yes, sure." Nick shook hands with my father. "Thanks for letting me come over."

Outside Nick and I sat down on two chairs I'd taken out of the garage. My mother hadn't put out the outdoor furniture yet, but I had intended to get some sun and had taken the two lawn chaises out in the morning.

"Your father's neat," Nick said, stretching out his legs the full length of the chaise. "He must have a lot of patience doing all that work himself. I'm still convinced he could make a lot more money if he wanted to. It's dumb to have just one of a kind."

"All you think about is money. You're used to everything coming off an assembly line. My father is an artist, not a manufacturer." Nick could be pretty dumb sometimes.

"If he could make a hundred or a thousand statues from one, what's wrong with that? My father would. My father's a gambler, he'd make a million of them." He laughed ruefully, "And probably lose his shirt. Like he does with his houses."

I looked at him in surprise. "I thought your father was very rich. You've got so much—your fantastic cars, all the things you have . . ."

"Don't believe it," he said carelessly. "It's all on paper. My father's always in over his head. He thinks he's going to make a million and he does it all on credit, and then something happens. The houses are built on landfill that's no good, or the roofs leak—there's always something. So he takes a loss and is further in debt. Although it's kind of exciting, and he stays very calm, one day he's going to crack up. That's what my mother says."

I was shocked that he would tell me these things. They didn't seem the sort of family confidences anyone would talk about, but Nick was very nonchalant. I guess it was so much a part of his life he didn't think about it, but it was new and strange to me. It was hard for me to imagine people living like that—in my own family my father hated owing money and we never bought anything on credit. I think my mother believes there is something low-class about buying on installment, that "quality" people bought only when they had the money to pay. I hoped she wouldn't find out about Mr. O'Carney; that would just be another reason for putting them down.

"It's a whole other world," I murmured.

Nick gave me a sharp look. "Yeah, you live a protected life. Must get boring."

He put me on the defensive. "It's not so bad." Then, suddenly I wanted to be more honest with him. "Sometimes, it's putrid," I said.

As if we both felt we'd said enough, we lay back and turned our faces to the sun. I took off my sneakers and socks and rolled up my jeans to get some sun on my legs. Nick had on sandals and no socks and just pulled up his jeans. It was nice lying in the sun with him next to me. I pretended that he was really my boyfriend and that we were on the deck of a ship going to some exotic island. I could almost feel the boat rocking under me.

Nick soon interrupted my lovely half-dream by standing up and saying that he had to go home. Then I remembered the concert tickets his mother had given me. "You want to go to a concert with me Friday night?" I asked.

"Who's playing?"

"No one you know." I thought for a minute of not telling him what kind of a concert it was but knew I couldn't get away with it. "It's classical music. Chamber music. It's good, you'll like it."

Nick wrinkled his nose. "What's chamber music? Sounds like something you play in the bathroom. Some of your highbrow stuff?"

"Give it a try. If you don't like it we can leave. Someone gave me the tickets so it won't cost us anything."

"Where's it going to be?"

"In the village. In the chapel of the Raleigh School."

"Oh, no. You won't get me into one of those prep school chapels again. I had enough of that in the school I was kicked out of. Those places give me the creeps. They make me feel like I'm going to a funeral."

"Come on, this one is okay, it's not gloomy. Try it."

"Okay. But remember, we walk out if it's what I expect it to be."

When Nick left I stayed out in the sun, and I wondered why I wanted him to go to the darn concert. I could have thrown the tickets away. I knew he probably would be bored stiff, yet I did know why I asked him—it was an excuse, a way to get him to go out with me. I figured he'd take it from there and hoped that going to a classical concert wouldn't kill off all my chances with him. Who knew, maybe by some miracle he'd enjoy it.

Julie said I shouldn't have asked him. "He just doesn't sound like the kind of guy you take to hear chamber music. Honestly, Alix, I don't know where your head is."

"I'm doing his mother a favor," I said.

"A lot of good that'll do you." We were on a field trip, riding in a bus. Our class was going to Sturbridge, a restored old village in Massachusetts. I'd been there with my parents, but I didn't mind going again. I liked the place, it was like stepping back into the seventeenth century.

When we got there we were supposed to stay in a group, but Julie and I trailed behind by ourselves. In the apothecary shop we examined bottles and jars of old-fashioned remedies for coughs and kidney ailments, lotions for removing warts, and whatnot.

After we finished looking at everything, we left and walked along the cobbled village street to a woodworking shop. Julie said she had to find a bathroom, and as I waited for her to return, I watched two men making duck decoys. I loved the

smell of the place; the fresh wood-shavings re-
minded me of my father's studio. The rest of our
class was there, and when they left I told Mrs.
Hammond, our teacher, that I was waiting for Julie and we'd catch up.

A boy from my school, Matthew Bardelli, stayed
behind, too. He was tall, and the tortoise-rimmed
glasses he wore gave him a serious look. Behind
his glasses he had bright blue eyes, and every once
in a while he flashed a sudden surprising smile. I
don't think we'd ever said more than hi to each
other, and we didn't speak now. He was talking
to the men working, asking them questions about
the tools they were using and what other things
they made. They showed him carvings of other
small animals and said that their crafts were sold
in the gift shop.

"My father uses wood a lot, too," I said, join-
ing in the conversation. "He's a sculptor."

"That's a little different from our carvings," one
of the men said, smiling.

"I know your father, at least I know his work,"
Matthew said shyly. "He's super. Someday I'm
going to buy something of his."

I was astonished. "You are? But they're expensive," I said bluntly.

"No they're not. Not for what they are."

"Oh, I know. I didn't mean they're not worth it. I only thought—"

"That I could never afford it," he finished my sentence. Our eyes met, and we both laughed. "I thought so too until I decided that was stupid," he said. "I work weekends, and I have a summer job. If I want a work of art I can buy it. I have friends who buy stereos for six or seven hundred dollars and motorcycles for even more. I'm going to buy a piece of sculpture. I saw the one I want in that gallery in the village. I'm thinking of putting a deposit on it so that no one else gets it first. It's the head of a woman with a scarf wound around her hair. I love just looking at it, it's so beautiful. She looks so real."

I looked at Matthew with new interest. "Are you really going to buy it? I'll tell my father, he'll be terribly pleased."

"It may take a long time."

"That doesn't matter." We stood side by side, neither of us knowing what to say next. Then Matthew said he'd better catch up with the class, I told him I'd wait for Julie, and he left.

I asked Julie about him when she finally came back. "Who is he? Of course I've seen him in class, but I don't know anything about him. Is he okay or is he a nerd?"

"I think he's okay," she said, not too convincingly. "I think his father left a few years ago, and his mother works in the paper factory. He's awfully quiet, a loner like you. I think he reads a lot." She looked at me thoughtfully. "He may be your type. Certainly more than Nick. Maybe you should cultivate him."

"He sounds dull," I said. "I don't want my type. He probably stays home and listens to Beethoven sonatas. I've had enough of that."

When Julie and I finally caught up with the others, I noticed that Matthew and I kept our distance from each other. It was as if there were a silent agreement that his wanting to buy a piece of my father's sculpture was no reason for us to become friends.

Six

FRIDAY NIGHT NICK PICKED ME UP IN HIS FA-
ther's sports car. How fabulous, I thought,
if only we were going to something more
exciting than a concert in the chapel at Raleigh.
It seemed to me that ever since I'd been three years
old I'd been taken to chamber music and symphony concerts, to the ballet, to museums, to art
shows. But I never went to a rock concert, a
professional baseball or football game, or played a
video game. I didn't really know any of the things
I should know. I wanted to learn them from Nick,
and here I was taking him to another dumb concert.

At first my mother had thought it was funny
that I had invited Nick to a classical concert. But

then she started to worry that I was taking his mother's hope seriously and was trying to be a good influence on him. I told her not to get upset, that someone had given me the tickets, and I didn't want to waste them. I didn't tell her who gave them to me.

When we arrived at the school and got out of the car, I noticed Nick was carrying something in a plastic bag. It looked like a small box. "What have you got there?" I asked.

Nick grinned and showed me a small radio with earphones. "You said if I got bored we could leave. I thought this would be better."

For a minute I didn't understand. Then it dawned on me that he intended to listen to his Walkman instead of the chamber music. I don't know how to describe my feelings. I was shocked; I thought it was wild and funny and awful at the same time. And I felt that in a way it was insulting, not only to the musicians but to me as well. I was embarrassed and angry that he could do such a thing. Yet I didn't know exactly what to say. I stayed very quiet, but I wasn't even sure if Nick noticed.

When we sat down, he made some cracks about the chapel giving him the creeps, and soon after the music started, he slipped the earphones on his head. I wanted to die of embarrassment, but no one sitting near us paid any attention. I sat frozen throughout the concert hardly listening to the music. Thank heavens it wasn't a long program, but it was the longest hour and a half I'd ever spent in my life.

I breathed a big sigh of relief when we went outside. I felt very mixed-up. Nick seemed absolutely at ease, as if everything was fine. Walking to the car he took my hand, and I thought I was a jerk not to feel fantastic with this terribly attractive boy and his fabulous sports car. Why should I care that he didn't want to listen to chamber music? After all, I didn't want to change him. Yet I had an uneasy feeling of something being wrong, as if some part of me was being threatened.

"You enjoy your music?" Nick asked amiably.

"Sure. You yours?"

"I listened to a basketball game. A good game. That place was stuffy, I've got to get that rarified air out of my lungs." He started up the car with a roar.

"Where are we going?" He hadn't turned in the direction of home.

"I don't know. Some place. Any place." He drove well but fast. I was nervous.

After a while he slowed down and turned to me with a grin. "I know what. We'll go to some midnight horror movie." He tapped his head. "A terrific idea," he said, bragging, "just what you need after that stuff."

"There are no midnight movies around here. You're in the sticks."

"That's what you think. You don't know half of what's around; there are movies over in Waterville. Friday and Saturday nights they have midnight shows."

"But that's sixty miles away. We can't go there."

"Why not? That's not far. In California we used to drive a hundred miles just to get good fried clams. It's nothing."

"How do you know about Waterville?" I asked, wondering what I'd tell my parents coming home so late. I decided to put that out of my mind.

"I find things out. I have my ways." He gave me a secretive grin.

"My parents are going to be worried," I said hesitatingly.

"They're probably sound asleep," he said confidently. "Have you ever been to a midnight movie before?" he asked gently.

"No."

"Then you're in for a treat. Now sit back and don't worry. The worst that can happen is that your parents may get mad, but they're not going to beat you up or do anything drastic. Just relax."

"Okay," I said. There was nothing I could do. I wasn't going to be a drag and beg him to take me home. Besides, I wanted to do things like other kids and this was it. I was excited about doing something that I knew my parents wouldn't approve of. If they got angry with me, so much the better.

We got to Waterville a little after eleven but the movie didn't start till twelve. Nick seemed to know his way around, and he drove a short way out of the center and down a small dead end road. Then he parked the car. I could feel myself tighten up and my heart beat faster. I didn't know what to expect—I wanted him to put his arms around me and kiss me but at the same time I was scared. I was afraid he would expect a lot more than I was ready for, and I didn't want to make a fool of myself.

Before he touched me, he opened the glove compartment and took out a small, leather-covered flask.

"What's that?" I asked nervously.

"Scotch." He opened the flask and handed it to me. "Have some."

I didn't tell him the strongest drink I'd ever had was a small glass of wine. I tipped the flask back and took a drink. It must have been very good Scotch, because it didn't burn the way I expected but went down as smooth as milk.

Nick took a long drink, closed the flask, and put it on the seat beside him. Then he turned to me. "Has a boy ever kissed you?" He had his hand on my hair, but I couldn't make out if he was serious or not.

"Of course. What do you think?"

"I think no one's kissed you the way I'm going to." He pulled me to him, and his mouth was on mine in a long, exploring kiss.

He was right. No one had ever kissed me that way before. It was as if some part of him was flowing into me and setting me afire. I knew that I would never be the same again.

He kissed me again and again and held me close. I was in a daze when he stopped. Then he picked up the flask and took another drink. He offered it to me, but I didn't want anything to erase the taste of him in my mouth.

"Mmm," he murmured, "you're a very passionate girl. I wouldn't have guessed."

I was in such a state of confusion I marveled at how relaxed and composed he was. He started up the car, turned on a cassette, and drove back to town with hardly a word. He just hummed along with the music. I felt that I had gotten past one hurdle. Nick hadn't tried anything I couldn't handle, and I hadn't made a fool of myself—yet. I felt as if I was walking a tightrope. I didn't want him to know just how unworldly I was, yet I wanted to be able to stop before I went over my head. I was scared he'd want me to go all the way with him, and I knew I didn't want to do that. The very idea terrified me. A boy like Nick, I felt, would take it for granted that a girl would go to bed with him. When he found out I wouldn't, that would be the end. I tried not to think about it.

The movie house was jammed with kids, and the audience was wilder than the show, which was saying a lot. The movie was a mixture of horror and sex, and the kids yelled and stomped and cheered like maniacs. Nick was as loud and crazy as any of them, but I thought it was pretty dumb and sat without opening my mouth.

"What's the matter with you?" Nick asked at one point. "Are you too sophisticated for this?"

"No. I think it's funny, but I don't feel like yelling."

"You think you're above this kind of thing, don't you?"

"No. Watch the movie; don't pick on me."

He put his arm around me and pinched my arm. "Hey, stop that," I did yell then. "You hurt me."

"I didn't think you'd feel it. I figured you were made of wood." He giggled, and I realized he was probably a little drunk. He'd taken a lot of swallows from that flask.

"Well, I'm not," I said.

"Come on, loosen up. Don't be so stiff." His arm around me was squeezing me.

"You didn't think I was stiff a little while ago. You said I was passionate." I tried to wriggle out of his grasp.

"That was then. This is now. You *are* made of wood—I'm getting splinters." He made a great show of taking away his hand and sucking on his fingers as if they hurt.

"You're behaving like an ass," I said. "If you don't want to watch the movie let's go." All the noise and cheering was getting on my nerves, and I was worried about driving home with Nick if he was drunk. "Let's go out and get some coffee."

"I don't want coffee. But let's go and get some more of that Scotch. It's good stuff." Nick got up and pulled me up after him. He staggered up the aisle waving to the kids on either side, and stopped once to kiss a girl on the cheek. The people around cheered.

When we got to the car I tried to take the flask away from him but he was stronger than I. "Keep your hands off that," he said, and grasped the flask firmly in his own hands. He threw his head back and drank. Then he put the ignition key in the lock, but I grabbed for it and took it out.

"I'll drive home," I said. I opened my door to walk around to the driver's side, but he held me back.

"I can drive." He said it quite calmly, and I wondered if he had been putting on some of his weird behavior. "I'm not drunk," he said emphatically.

"You've been acting as if you were."

He pulled me toward him. "Loosen up. Don't be so stiff." Then he held my face away so that he could study it. "You're so pretty, but you don't know how to have any fun." When he started to sing at the top of his voice, I knew he was drunk.

"I'm going to drive," I said again. I didn't tell him I didn't have a license yet. I knew how to drive and figured I was better off taking a chance driving without a license than driving with someone who had had too much to drink.

Nick turned to me and grinned. "Sure, you drive," he said. "I'm crocked. Smashed. Too bad, with a nice, innocent girl like you. Shouldn't have done it, never get drunk with a nice girl, very foolish, spoil everything. Nick, you've got no sense . . ." He went on talking to himself and was really quite funny, as he moved over and let me get into the driver's seat.

When he wasn't conducting his monologue about nice, pretty girls and drinking, he sang until we got home. With great relief, I pulled the car into his driveway. "Are you going to be okay?" I asked.

"Me? Sure, I'm fine. I'm terrific." He stumbled out of the car and made a low bow. "You're a beautiful girl. A beautiful driver. I'll hire you to be my chauffeur. Chauffeur and mistress." He laughed outrageously, and I was afraid he'd wake up his family. It was very late and the house was dark.

"Do you want me to take you inside?"

"I'll take you." He put out his arm for me to take.

I walked him up to his front door. It had been left unlocked, and I opened it, and we went inside. There was a light on in the hall so I figured he'd be able to get to his room. As I turned to leave, he grabbed me to him and kissed me. In spite of everything my body responded to his, and I wondered what might have happened if he hadn't gotten drunk. Part of me was relieved and part of me wished he had stayed sober.

The night was pitch-black, and I felt my way across the road. However, my parents had left the outside light on, so once I reached our driveway I made my way easily to the house. I stopped outside the door. If they were still up, I'd be in for it. I didn't have my watch on but I knew it had to be terribly late. I panicked. What a fool I was not to have called them at least. But if I had, they would have said to come home.

I stood outside several minutes before I got up the courage to open the door. They were waiting for me.

I'd never seen my father look that way. He was white and tense, his face so pale he looked sick, and his hands were clenched. My mother was stretched out on the sofa with the heating pad that she held to her head when she had a migraine.

They were both in bathrobes. My mother got almost hysterical when she saw me and kept saying, "Thank God you're all right, thank God . . ."

"If it weren't for that boy's parents we'd be

dragging the river for you by now," my father said.

"What have they got to do with it?" I was bewildered.

"Naturally we called them. They kept telling us not to worry, that for Nick to be out this late on a date was natural. I don't understand those people, I just don't understand." My father kept shaking his head in disbelief. "We're not used to this, Alix. We don't even know what to say to you." My father sat down heavily in his armchair and leaned forward toward where I was standing by the fireplace. "Why didn't you call us? Why? It would have been so easy for you to do."

"I was afraid you'd tell me to come right home," I said. "Nick suggested a movie after the concert, and that's where we were. We came home right after the movie."

"A movie until three in the morning?" My mother looked at me questioningly. "I never expected you to lie to us."

"I'm not lying. It was a midnight movie. They have them over in Waterville, all the kids go."

"You went way over to *Waterville?*" She was shocked.

"It's not that far."

My parents looked at each other despairingly. They looked so miserable, they made me feel

68

horrible. If they had scolded me, yelled at me, I would have felt better. This way I knew I'd done something they didn't know how to cope with, and they were frightened. "I'm sorry," I said. "I'm very sorry."

"Did you have a good time?" My mother tried to smile weakly.

"Pretty good." I couldn't bear to tell them I'd had a terrible time, it would only make them feel worse. "It was fun."

"Do you really like that boy?" my mother asked sincerely.

"Yes, I like him very much." Again I felt swept with guilt. What would she think if she knew that what I really liked was for him to touch me, to kiss me? That he made me feel dangerously alive. Suddenly my parents and I were worlds apart, and the new gulf between us made me feel sad.

"Would you like some hot cocoa?" she asked.

"No, thanks. I think I'll go to bed. I'm very sorry." I kissed them both, and their eyes followed me out of the room. I went up to my room feeling that I had lost something irretrievable, something I had left behind in that room with my stunned parents.

Seven

THE DATE WITH NICK HAD BEEN SO PECU-
liar I didn't know how things were between us. I hated the uncertainty, not
knowing if he liked me, if he'd call me again, or
if I should call and ask him how he was. I wasn't
even sure how I felt about him. Thinking about
him made me nervous, yet I wanted to see him
again because he was exciting. I kept hoping I'd
see him going in or out, but several days went by
and there wasn't a sign of him. Since school was
out for the summer, I didn't see Eileen at the bus
stop, so I couldn't try prying anything out of her.

However, about a week after that Friday night,
I saw her outside with her bike, and in despera-
tion, I ran out to catch her. "Hi, how's it going?"
I asked. "I haven't seen you around lately. In fact,

I haven't seen any of your family. Where's your brother? Is he away?" I hoped I sounded casual.

She gave me a sharp look. "No, he's here. He doesn't get up till twelve or one o'clock. Sometimes later. That's because he doesn't come home until three or four in the morning. My mom's pretty mad. He's got a girl in the village he sees."

"Oh." My heart sank. "That's nice for him. Anyone I know?" It was humiliating to be asking her but I had to know. I tried to ignore the knowing glint in her eyes.

"I doubt it. You wouldn't know her, she's a townie. My mother says she's a bum."

I didn't have the courage to ask for her name. I'd heard enough to send me to the pits. I wasn't dumb enough to think he'd really fall for me, but I didn't expect to be dropped so fast. "Tell him I said hello." I had the foolish notion that that might let her think I didn't care about Nick and his girl.

But Eileen was too sharp. "Maybe he'll get tired of her," she said. "He never sticks with any girl for long."

"I'm sure of that," I said glibly, her sympathy being about the last thing in the world I wanted.

So that was that. My little venture into that exciting world I didn't know about was over.

*   *   *

"I live in a cocoon," I said to Julie later that day as we were having sodas in the village. "I'll never get out of it."

"You never should have taken him to that concert. That was a mistake."

"I know," I said glumly. "But I don't think it would have made any difference. I'm a dud, and there's nothing I can do about it. He thinks I'm just a kid, and I'm sure he knows I'm a virgin. Heck, I'd never really been kissed his way before, and I let him know it. I blew it for sure."

"Nick was wrong for you, but there are others. What about that Matthew Bardelli? He's more your type."

"I told you, I don't want my type," I said fiercely. "I don't like my type. I don't even want to be my type. It's my parents' fault, they brought me up all wrong."

Julie didn't say anything, but I was sure she was thinking it's too late now to change that.

That's what worried me, too. I was only fifteen years old, but I felt my life was already cast in a terrible, dull mold. Obviously I didn't appeal to exciting guys like Nick, and I could see endless days, months, and years ahead of watching other people have passionate love affairs, lead fantastically interesting lives while I lived a ghastly, solitary existence, a weird old lady surrounded by books and music—and emptiness.

Something terrible happened. I began to hate my parents. It was as if suddenly a curtain had been lifted, and I saw them as characters in a play on stage. They were strangers, not my parents, not even real people. Everything they did now got on my nerves: watching my father mix a salad dressing as if he were performing a religious ritual, measuring, smelling, tasting; seeing my mother arrange the magazines on the table, placing each one in an exact position; listening to them dissect a concert they'd heard, the violin too sharp, the oboe too soft, the percussion instruments too loud. The importance they attached to everything they did, every word they said, suddenly became irritating and ridiculous.

Sitting at the dinner table with them was the worst. I couldn't remember why I used to enjoy our dinners. Now I dreaded each meal and asked to be excused without waiting for dessert.

A few days after Eileen had told me about Nick and his new girl, Mrs. O'Carney came over to see my mother. It was in the middle of the afternoon and I was home. She appeared wearing her usual silly high-heeled shoes and a sleeveless pink shift.

She offered my mother a bag of bulbs she was carrying. "I ordered too many," she said, coming inside when my mother opened the door, "and I'd just love you to have these. I can't guarantee the colors, they're all mixed up, but they're beautiful tulips. She peered through the doorway from the hall into the living room. "Your house is so pretty, and those beautiful figures that your husband makes. Nick thinks he's marvelous. It must be wonderful living with an artist. I'd just love to see your house. I do love old houses, but I'll never get a chance to live in one, not with a builder for a husband . . ." She gave a high little laugh.

My mother had no choice but to take her through the downstairs where she ooh'd and aah'd over the fireplaces and antiques. "I just love old things, don't you?"

My mother smiled weakly.

"There's a little shop with the cutest things in the new shopping mall," Mrs. O'Carney babbled on, "full of adorable vases and lamps. Have you been there? The mall has everything—a huge supermarket, and discount housewares stores, just acres of merchandise. I could spend weeks there. If you like I'll take you over one afternoon. There's a darling tearoom where we could have lunch." She looked at my mother wistfully.

"That's very kind, but I rarely go out for lunch. It interrupts my workday. Thank you so much for the bulbs," my mother said as she led Mrs. O'Carney to the door, rather hastily, I thought. "It was nice of you to think of me. I'm sure we'll enjoy them."

My mother closed the door firmly behind our neighbor and gave a deep sigh. "What a dreadful woman. I can't stand that voice of hers and her silly little laugh."

Hearing her say this, I exploded. "You don't even know her," I yelled. All my pent-up feelings had to get out. "She may be a wonderful person for all you know. You're a snob. She wants to be friendly, she's a neighbor, and you just give her the cold shoulder. All your phony gracious living is a fake. What's so gracious about being snobby with a neighbor because you don't like her voice or her laugh?"

My mother stared at me in astonishment, and I stared back. It was as if I wanted to hit back for every museum I'd been dragged to, every concert, every ballet. What was the good of all that stuff when she couldn't be decent to another human being?

"I don't know what's got into you," my mother said, visibly trying to remain calm. "I am not a snob, and there is no reason in the world why I have to make friends with someone just because they happen to live next door. Mrs. O'Carney and I have absolutely nothing in common. I can still choose my friends and just because you imagine you have a crush on that son of hers, I don't have to lower *my* standards."

"What do you mean, imagine?"

"I can't believe you seriously like him. I respect you too much for that." My mother smiled at me indulgently.

"Whether I do or not has nothing to do with it," I said coldly. "And my standards are just as good as yours. You and Dad think you're so special. Well, I don't want to be special. You have an ordinary daughter whether you like it or not."

With that I marched out of the house and walked down the road. I was mad. It was their fault I'd lost Nick, their fault I didn't have any friends except Julie, their fault I wasn't going out and having a good time like other girls.

I wanted to do something to show them just how much I hated their world, but I didn't know what to do. When I did think of something, naturally, it was something silly.

After I came back home, I sat outside for a while. When I finally went back into the house my mother was in the kitchen. She had a gourmet cookbook propped up on the counter and was boning a chicken. "Don't make any supper for me," I said, "I'm going to McDonald's for a hamburger and French fries."

My mother couldn't hide her smile. "That's pretty silly, isn't it?"

"Maybe it is. I don't care. I want to be silly. I'm going whether it is or not."

"You'll miss a good meal. And how do you plan to get there?" McDonald's was up off the highway, a few miles away.

"I'll ride my bike."

I had never done anything like this before in my life, and I had to admit I did feel foolish. Going to McDonald's didn't seem like much of a rebellion. Especially alone, on a bike. If I had been running away someplace exciting with Nick, it would mean something. But I got on my bike and pedaled off anyway. I wasn't even hungry by the time I got to the highway, but I could see the McDonald's sign, so I went inside.

The place wasn't very crowded, and I got my hamburger, French fries, and a soda and sat down at a table by myself. I was munching away wondering what I was doing there when Nick and a girl came in. They were holding hands, and I knew immediately she was his new girl. She was quite pretty with curly dark hair, a small, pale face, and large brown eyes. Heavy black eyeliner dwarfed the rest of her features so that she looked all eyes.

Nick saw me and waved hello. A bunch of kids came in when they did, and by the time Nick and his girl had their food there were no empty tables. They came over toward me, and Nick looked around hesitatingly, then asked if they could sit with me.

"Sure," I said, wishing I was a million miles away. I couldn't believe this was happening. I had come away to be alone, to figure out how I was going to get over Nick, get out of my parents' clutches, to change my life-style, and here I was having supper with him and his girl. Surely there was a hex on me.

Nick introduced Mary Jane Thompson, and they sat down. She smiled hello, and then hardly said a word the rest of the meal. She kept looking over to Nick either to make sure he was there, or, I thought, to have his approval. She looked older than he, with very long red nails, a silky blouse and no bra, very tight jeans and high heels, but when she looked at Nick she seemed unsure and young. I wondered if he made every girl feel that way.

Nick did most of the talking. He told Mary Jane all about what my parents did, what our house looked like, and, of all silly things, how we didn't have a television. I was embarrassed and began to get annoyed until I realized that he was nervously making conversation. He was trying to get across to her that I wasn't a girlfriend of his and also in a funny way bragging that he and his family knew arty people like us. The latter reason struck me as so ironic, I wanted to laugh.

The two of them were sitting together opposite me, and they kept touching each other as if they couldn't keep their hands quiet. I didn't want to stare at Mary Jane, but I glanced at her whenever she turned to look at Nick. Looking at her pale, pretty face, I could see that she had a sensuality and a tenseness that I imagined could be passionate when she let herself go. She was obviously crazy about him.

I finished, got up, and left before they did. Outside I didn't know what to do. I didn't feel like going home yet, but I didn't want to be sitting there when they came out, so I rode off the highway onto a side road. I had never felt really jealous of anyone before so it took me a while to realize what my feeling of depression and hurt actually was. I discovered, too, that I wasn't only jealous of Mary Jane, I was jealous of the two of them, of what they had and I didn't. The way they looked at each other, the way they touched—they seemed so happy together and obviously in love. I felt miserable—so awkward and self-conscious and juvenile. I hated myself more than ever.

My father was on his way out when I got home. "Did you enjoy your supper?" he asked.

"It was all right."

"There's some delicious chicken left if you want some," he said. "You don't have to be ashamed to eat it."

"I'm not ashamed. Not of eating in McDonald's either. The only thing I'm ashamed of is being so ignorant, and that's not my fault."

"You have nothing to be ashamed of," my father said earnestly. "You know more than most girls your age. You are far from ignorant. You can be proud of what you know."

"That's what you think. I don't know anything. You think the girls and boys in my class talk about Renaissance music, or abstract art or what George Eliot wrote over a hundred years ago? You're the ones who are ignorant, you and Mom." I glared at him.

"Really? What's so great about the kids in your class with their junk food and junk learning and junk electronic games? Tell me. What are they accomplishing, do you think they're going to make the world any better when they grow up?" My father was standing in the doorway, half in and half out.

"I don't see you and Mom, or people like you, doing any more. Who sees your sculpture anyway? You and a handful of people. And Mom's weaving? Only a few rich people who can afford to buy it." I was being cruel and I knew it.

My father's face turned white. "You *are* ignorant," he said pityingly. "You don't know very much, and I guess your mother and I have failed in teaching you. You don't know anything about the satisfaction in making something, in doing it yourself, in doing something well. Listen, my dear daughter. Our society needs people like us. Like you, too. There are thousands—millions—of people with their fast food, tacky houses, cheap art; but we are getting fewer and fewer . . . the people who care about physical beauty, the environment, our homes, the *quality* of our lives. Don't put us down, and don't put yourself down in order to be one of the crowd. You're beginning to sound just like your friend Nick. You're starting to see everything in dollars and cents only. I feel sorry for you."

He went out of the door and left me with tears

blinding my eyes. I felt both betrayed and as if I had done the betraying. I stood in the hallway for a few minutes before going up to my room. I thought maybe he would come back, and he would hug me and everything would be all right. But he didn't. I could hear him start up the car and drive away. My father and I had never spoken to each other that way before. I felt that I had crossed a bridge and there was no going back.

Later when my father came home I was up in my room, and I heard him talking to someone. A moment later my mother called, "Alix, come down. A friend of yours is here."

For a minute I thought it was Nick and my heart stopped, but I realized that it couldn't be.

Nevertheless, I was really surprised to find Matthew Bardelli in the living room with my parents. Standing over by the fireplace, he looked taller and skinnier than ever.

"Matthew is buying one of my pieces," my father said, "and I brought him home to see what I have in the studio."

"I know, he told me he was. You said you were going to leave a deposit," I said, turning to him.

"That's what I did. But your father was very kind and let me take it. I have it in the car. I'm terribly excited, I thought I'd have to wait months for it. I'll pay it off as fast as I can. I've never owned anything like this before." His face was beaming.

"I hope it's the first of many." I could see my father was terribly pleased. "I'm flattered that a young man like you wants to spend his hard-earned money on something I made. It's a great compliment." He threw me a meaningful glance. "Alix was saying only a little while ago that people her own age don't give a hang about art."

"I guess a lot of them don't," Matthew said. "They probably think I'm a weirdo. Maybe I am, but I don't care."

"Good for you," my mother said. "Not everyone has to go with the crowd."

I felt that the three of them were ganging up against me. "Are you going out to the studio?" I asked abruptly.

"I was making some tea," my mother said. "Or would you rather have a soda?" she asked Matthew.

"No, tea is fine."

They both thought Matthew was wonderful, and I found that highly irritating. Just because he bought a piece of my father's sculpture didn't make him so special.

We sat around drinking tea, and Matthew talked

about his plans for the summer. His hobby was archaeology, and he told them how he hoped to spend a few weeks in August at the American-Indian Institute in Connecticut and work on some digs over at Lake Waramaug.

"I was there a couple of years ago," he said. "It was awfully exciting. You never know what you're going to find. We found some beautiful arrowheads and pieces of pottery. They have one of the pieces I found in their museum collection; it makes me feel real good when I see it there."

I had nothing against Matthew, but I hated the way my parents fawned over him and were so impressed. I could just see the wheels in their minds go round, thinking, Now why doesn't Alix go out with an interesting boy like this?

Why? I could tell them. It wasn't Matthew's fault, but he was their kind, and I didn't want to be like them. I didn't want to be part of their intellectual, antiseptic existence. I wanted Life with a capital L. Lots of noise and people, hustle and bustle.

Before Matthew left after touring my father's studio, he asked me if I wanted to drive over one Sunday to Music Mountain for a concert. "They have them quite often. We could take a picnic lunch."

I felt he was asking me just to be polite, so I said I'd see. "Depends on when it would be."

"I'll look up the programs and give you a call," he said.

The minute he left I went up to my room before I had to listen to my parents say again what a nice boy Matthew was. I wanted to think about Nick and Mary Jane. I wondered what they were doing. Making love, no doubt, and thinking about them gave me that sinking feeling of desolation again. I don't even know if it was jealousy but more the thought that everyone else was out there having an exciting, beautiful time, and that I never would. I was going to turn middle-aged before I ever had any fun being young.

Eight

THE NEXT DAY I WENT OVER TO JULIE'S HOUSE to find out what I could about Mary Jane. Julie's mother worked in the bank in town and brought home all the gossip.

"Yes, I know who she is," Julie said, "and I'm not surprised Nick's going with her." She looked at me sympathetically. "She's at least eighteen if not nineteen, and she's been around. Her mother ran away with someone a few years ago, and her father hasn't been home for months. She lives with an aunt, I think, unless she's shacking up with someone. Forget about Nick and Mary Jane, they're not for you, Alix."

"I can't forget about them. I keep wondering if I should have acted differently with Nick. I should

have been sexier and not let him know how innocent I am. But he probably would have gotten
bored with me anyway. It's awful, Julie, not
knowing how to be and what to do. I don't even
know what's right and wrong. Nick and that girl
looked so happy together, that's really what made
me jealous. If I could be that way with a boy, I
don't think I'd care about anything else."

"You're not the only one," Julie said. We were
out in her backyard sitting in her swing. "You
think I know all the time? I'm going with Greg
Moore now, and I know that sooner or later the
same question is going to come up. It's come up
already—do we make love or don't we? I'm not a
brain like you, and I've been with boys more, but
that doesn't make it any easier. I like Greg, a lot,
but I get terribly nervous when I think of sleep-
ing with him. Every night that I come home and
I've managed not to, I feel, Thank God I'm still
safe. But it's a terrible drag. I mean, Greg gets
me awfully excited. Consider yourself lucky that
you haven't got a boyfriend. Maybe when you're
older it'll be easier."

"That's a lousy prospect," I said glumly, giving
the swing a hard push with my foot. "I won't know
anymore then than I do now. How am I going to
learn anything? Kids who never heard a sym-

phony know more than I do, and I'm supposed to be so educated. The whole thing's a farce. The things you really need to learn about no one teaches you."

We sat swinging, each nursing our misery, until we looked at each other's mournful faces and burst out laughing. That was the great part about Julie, we could laugh together so easily.

But when I left her, the depression I'd felt was still there. Instead of walking on the hot road I took a path through the woods where it was cool. The bugs weren't too bad, and the huge silence was restful. I felt at home in these woods, and I never thought about being frightened. Yet I was scared stiff when I heard the strange sound of someone crying. At first I thought it was an animal, maybe caught in a stupid trap someone had put out, but then as I heard real sobs, I knew it was a person.

That frightened me more. I could deal with a hurt animal, but I was afraid of finding someone who was bloody or dying. Yet instinctively I ran down the path toward the sounds. I was stunned to see Eileen O'Carney sitting on the ground, her legs crossed under her, openly crying. She didn't cover her face with her hands, they were twisting a red bandana in anguish.

"Eileen," I called out to her softly so I wouldn't frighten her. "Eileen . . . it's me, Alix."

Her face was so sad, and she just looked at me without speaking.

"Are you all right? Did you fall? What's the matter?"

She kept looking at me dumbly. "I'm okay," she mumbled. "I came out here to cry, that's all."

"Can I do anything?"

She shook her head. "No one can do anything."

"You sound awful. What happened?" I was standing near her, and I knelt down so I wouldn't be towering above her.

"I don't know . . ." She started to cry again. "It's my parents, I'm scared they're going to get a divorce. They had a terrible fight. They've had them before, but this one was worse."

"Maybe it just sounded worse," I said. "Lots of parents fight. It doesn't mean anything."

"They say terrible things. They fight mostly about money. I hate it. Sometimes I wish we didn't have any money."

"I don't think you'd like that. Think of all the fantastic things you have. You like them, don't you?"

"Yes, sure, but I don't have to have them. My

father buys things, and then they fight because he hasn't got the money to pay for them. That's what gets my mother mad."

She looked so small and miserable. I wanted to comfort her, but I didn't know what to say. I felt very sorry for her.

"Do your parents fight?" she asked me.

I wished I could have said yes. "No, they don't," I said truthfully. "Sometimes I wish they would. Everything in our house is so quiet. It's funny, isn't it? You don't want your parents to fight, and I wish mine would." I tried to make her laugh but she just looked sadder. "How's your brother?" I asked to change the subject. "I haven't seen him around much lately."

"He's never home," Eileen said bitterly. "He's busy with his girlfriend."

"Mary Jane? Do you like her?" I was tormenting myself.

"She's okay. She paints nice pictures."

"She paints?" I was thunderstruck. "Where did you see her pictures?"

"Nick brought some home to show my mother. He wants Mary Jane to put them in an art show. Nick thinks she should go to art school. My mother wanted to show them to your father, but Nick took them back, I don't know why."

"Mary Jane can take them to an art gallery herself, she doesn't need my father." I had an image of childish little landscapes that would have embarrassed my father.

The idea of Mary Jane painting was bizarre, completely out of character. It seemed stupid of Nick to think that just anyone could get displayed in an art show. People worked for years to even get a gallery to represent them. I felt even more jealous. Knowing that Mary Jane was a girl from town with a bad reputation didn't bother me as much as learning that she wanted to be an artist and that Nick was trying to help her. If he could be interested in a girl that way, why not me?

Eileen and I walked the rest of the way home together, both of us depressed. Since misery loves company I felt closer to her.

A call from Matthew later that day didn't cheer me up. Going to a concert with him wasn't my idea of an exciting date. He said there was a good Beethoven and Brahms program that Sunday and asked if I would like to go with him. I didn't have anything else to do, so I said yes and agreed to make a picnic lunch.

During the week I saw Nick and Mary Jane several times—on his motorcycle, her hair flying, or in the sports car, Nick's arm around her. They were always laughing and I was sick with envy. I felt such a failure. I'd had my chance with him—he lived right across the way, he'd started out so friendly, he'd asked me out—but I blew it. I'd done everything wrong because *I* was wrong, a number-one misfit.

The more I thought about Nick and Mary Jane the more I wished I weren't going to the concert with Matthew. By comparison it seemed so dull and stodgy, like something old people would do. So I was not in a good mood on Saturday when my mother asked me what she should make for our picnic lunch.

"I don't care," I told her. "I can make some peanut butter sandwiches."

"Oh, no. Take something more festive than that. I have a hunch Matthew would appreciate something nice." My mother's eyes sparkled and I realized she was excited about my date with Matthew. Naturally my reaction was to loathe it more than ever.

"I'm not about to fuss for Matthew Bardelli. As a matter of fact, I'm sorry I said I'd go with him. I expect to be bored stiff."

My mother looked annoyed. I'd never talked to her like that before, and I was as surprised as she was.

"What on earth is the matter with you, darling? I don't know what has come over you. Something has happened to you, and I don't think I like it. You're changing. The last thing in the world I ever expected was for you to turn into a typical hostile teenager."

"I'm not hostile," I said haughtily. "You and Dad have made a mess of bringing me up, and I'm just discovering it. You've kept me from being like other girls, from having fun, from being normal."

"You were a perfectly happy girl until that boy moved in next door. He and his dreadful family. All these new ideas you have came directly from them. I don't understand how a girl brought up as you've been, with an appreciation of the finer things in life, could fall for their rubbish." It was the closest thing to anger I'd ever seen in my mother.

"You think people who don't like the same things you do are rubbish. You think you're better than other people. You turn up your nose at people who live in developments and eat in fast-food places and their kids who listen to rock. Who are you to say you're more refined than they are? And who cares? I want to be like those people and do all the things other kids do." We glared at each other.

Then all the anger seemed to drain out of my mother. "That was quite a speech," she said limply. "I guess your father and I have failed." She let out a deep sigh. "We've spent a good deal of time and effort, and money, too, to give you advantages, to expose you to fine music, art, the things we believe are worthwhile. It is sad to see that it was wasted, that you are eager to trade in your appreciation of good music, ballet, and such for a lot of junk because you think it's stylish. You have learned to enjoy things that are enduring, while the other stuff—the video games and all—are fads. Five years from now, probably even less, there will be something different."

"But I don't want to be like you two," I cried out. "I don't mean that I don't admire you," I said in a quieter tone, "but I want different things."

As I finished, my mother turned away, and I was afraid she was crying. But then she straightened up and said briskly, "Now I have to go shopping, and if you will tell me what you want for lunch I'll get it."

"I don't care. Get whatever you want."

Of course she had succeeded in making me feel awful. After she left I felt like crying, but I couldn't even do that.

I hated being on the outs with my parents. At

dinner that night I could tell that my mother had reported our conversation to my father. They were both trying hard to connect with me. My mother talked about a great dress she wanted me to try on that she'd seen in the Indian shop, and my father asked if I wanted to go to a movie in the village after dinner while they were visiting some friends. He even asked if I wanted to invite Nick to join me.

"I'm sure he's busy," I said, not admitting that that would be the last thing I'd want to do. "Besides the movie is some dumb thing you and Mom wouldn't really want me to see."

"How do you know? We like a lot of things," my father grinned at me cheerfully.

"You wouldn't like this one," I said. It was a silly situation comedy that I didn't even want to see.

"Then what would you like to do this evening?"

"Nothing, thanks. I have some library books I can read."

I caught them exchanging glances, and I felt sorry and embarrassed. I really didn't expect them to change, and I wasn't sure I wanted them to. What I couldn't say to either one of them was that I wasn't looking for them to please me, to do things for me. That wouldn't solve anything. I wanted my own friends and to find out for myself the things I wanted to do.

My father finally asked if I'd like to come with them, and again I said no. "You two go. I'd rather stay home."

I was afraid they were going to stay home with me, but I finally persuaded them I felt like being alone. They both looked sad and worried when they left, but I sighed with relief.

I didn't do much reading. Mainly I lay on my bed gazing up at the ceiling. I almost wished I'd never laid eyes on the O'Carneys and that they had stayed in California. Knowing them, meeting Nick, *had* changed me, although I'd begun to feel restless even before that.

I kept my door closed when I heard my parents come home. Ordinarily, if I hadn't been with them, I would have gone down and joined them in the kitchen for a cup of herbal tea. But I didn't answer my mother when she called, and I turned off my light before they came upstairs. Let them think I was sound asleep. Finally I fell into a restless sleep. When I woke up in the morning, my bed was a mess from all my twisting and turning.

My mother had made barbecued chicken for our picnic. I packed bread and butter, tomatoes, fruit, and cheese. Whether I liked it or not, I had an elegant lunch. If I had been going with Nick I would have been excited, but then he wouldn't be going on a picnic to Music Mountain.

Matthew picked me up around eleven. He had a tape deck in his car and we drove off to the sound of a Chopin sonata. That was fine with me since I didn't have to make conversation. Matthew was quiet, too, so I sat back in my seat to think about Nick. That wasn't such a good idea, though, since I couldn't think of him without seeing him with Mary Jane.

We were both hungry when we got to Music Mountain, so we found a shady spot to eat, away from other picnickers. My mother had put a red-checkered tablecloth in the lunch basket, and I spread that on the grass and took out our food.

"Wow, what a feast," Matthew said. "I knew you weren't the peanut butter-and-jelly type. I knew what I was doing when I asked you to bring the lunch."

I had to smile. He didn't know how close he'd come to getting peanut butter. "You can thank my mother. This is all her idea." We were both chewing on drumsticks.

"Your parents are super. Really great."

"They're okay."

He looked up at me, questioningly. "You don't think so? You seem such a together family."

"I said they were all right." I guess my voice sounded hostile.

"Okay. I guess other people's parents always seem better than your own."

"Don't you like yours?"

"I only have my mother. I haven't seen my father for about two years. They're divorced."

"I'm sorry."

"You don't have to be. They didn't get along. I think my mother's better off. She gets lonely, but that's better than being miserable."

"Maybe I am lucky," I said. "My parents never fight. Sometimes I wish they would."

Matthew laughed. "Don't wish that on yourself. It's no good; it's rotten. It's no fun to come home and find your mom bawling her head off and know that your father's taken off and probably won't be home until the next morning."

"It does sound lousy. I can see why you're glad he's gone."

"It's a relief. He didn't think much of me anyway. I'm not big on athletics—he's a baseball fan—and he was not what I'd call enthusiastic about my plans."

"Like what?" I was polite, but I can't say I was wildly interested in Matthew. My mind kept wandering, wondering what I was doing there with him.

His face had an eager look when he turned to

me. "You really want to know? I'm going to be an environmentalist. I'm going to work somewhere trying to clean up this old planet. I figure that if we don't get blown up by a nuclear bomb, we're going to die of pollution unless we do something about it. So that's what I intend to do."

"That's great." I realized my voice didn't sound very enthusiastic, but I couldn't help it. All I could think of was that my parents would adore Matthew now, and that was enough to put me off him. "I guess we should be going inside. I think the concert's going to start soon," I said, and gathered up our picnic.

While we listened to the music Matthew tried to take my hand, but I kept my hands folded in my lap. I could feel him looking at me, but I just stared ahead at the musicians. When the intermission came, we went outside.

"Are you enjoying the music?" Matthew asked.

"It's okay."

"What's the matter with you? Are you all right? You don't look very happy."

"I'm not. Everything is rotten," I said unexpectedly.

Behind his glasses, Matthew narrowed his eyes and frowned. "What's eating you? It's a gorgeous day, we're here in a fabulous place listening to good music. What's wrong?"

"I don't know . . . I'm sorry. I don't want to spoil your day."

"You don't like me, do you? Why'd you come with me anyway?" He was getting angry.

"I shouldn't have. I'm very sorry. I guess I came to please my parents. I'm in love, that's the trouble," I blurted out in a burst of confidence.

"Great. Then why aren't you with whatever character you're in love with?"

"He doesn't give a hang about me. I shouldn't have come with you." I felt terrible.

"You're darn right you shouldn't have."

He walked away a few feet down a path. I followed after him. "I'm sorry if I'm spoiling your day."

"Think nothing of it," he said sarcastically. "Do you want to tell me who this great guy is?"

"Not really. Besides, you probably wouldn't like him. My parents don't. They think he's vulgar, lowbrow. He is, kind of."

"What do you see in him?"

"I like him. He's sexy, different, does what he wants. Kind of crazy. He's everything I'm not." I noticed Matthew had long lashes, the kind a girl would love to have.

He looked at me from under them. "You have a problem," he said flatly. "Obviously he's not your type. Except for the sexy part."

"Why? You think I'm sexy?"

"Possibly. I wouldn't know whether you are or not. Not until I'd kissed you."

"Is that a test?"

"Usually. Want to find out?"

"No thank you. Certainly not here, with all these people around."

"Too bad. I thought you wanted to be daring. Be different, do what you want, not care what people thought." Now I realized that he hadn't been serious. He was treating me like a spoiled kid.

"I'll never be that kind of person," I said quietly. "You won't either."

He bristled at that. "That's what you think. I am right now. You're too dumb to know it. I wouldn't be here with you if I weren't. I don't know any other boy who would have asked you to hear a concert up here. They'd take you to rock music or country singing, something that's 'in.' I don't give a darn about the top ten or the newest band. I like what I like, and I don't care what people think. Come on," he said brusquely, "let's go, the music is starting."

The concert hall was a large, airy, simple room, painted white and with wide, tall windows. I was glad to go back inside and to sit and listen to the music and feel the warmth of the sun streaming in through the open windows. The music made me feel sad and to long to be in love with someone who loved me back. Just thinking about being in love made me think of Nick. Being with him was like being with a tightly wound-up spring, and the excitement was not knowing when the spring would suddenly be released and the unexpected come bursting forth.

Sitting next to Matthew I could sense his anger and annoyance with me. He sat looking straight ahead as if nothing in the world mattered except the music. Somehow I doubted that was true, but I was in no mood to make any gesture toward him. I was irritated with myself as well as with him. I looked around at the audience, mostly old ladies—only a few young people—and I thought, What am I doing here? I longed to get out and run across the fields. I wanted to shake up that serious, precious group who were so like my parents, and Matthew was one of them.

As soon as the concert ended, Matthew and I walked to the car silently. He drove me straight home and we hardly said a word to each other. At my house I said a polite thank you and good-bye; he said good-bye, and that was that.

"How was it? Did you have a good time?" My mother greeted me eagerly.

"It was all right," I said coolly.

She gave my father an uneasy look. "Did Matthew like the lunch?"

"I guess so." I was as mean to them as I had been to Matthew, but I couldn't stop myself. I quickly excused myself and went up to my room feeling like a heel, but angry and frustrated at the same time.

Nine

THE LAUNDROMAT SEEMED TO BE AN AUSPI-
cious place for me. I was there on Monday, the day after the concert, and Matthew was on my mind. Actually, I had felt uncomfortable all evening thinking about the day and
how badly I'd behaved. While Matthew had kept
his distance, he had been pretty decent. He could
have really let me have it; while he might never
want to see me again, I felt I owed him an apology.

He worked down the block in a stationery store,
so after I put the clothes in the machines, I went
over there. The store was empty. Matthew's boss
was in the back, and Matthew was putting a bunch
of pads away on a shelf. He turned around and
looked surprised when he saw me.

"Can I get you something?" he asked like I was a customer he'd never seen before.

"No, thank you. I came to see you. I was down the street at the laundromat, and I was thinking . . ." It was hard for me to get out what I wanted to say. He kept looking at me with an expressionless face. "I'm sorry about yesterday. I'm sorry I wasn't any fun and that I spoiled your day."

"You didn't spoil my day," he said coolly. "I enjoyed the music—I like going there, even by myself, so it didn't matter. Besides," he added with a half-smile, "the lunch was good."

"You can thank my mother for that," I said.

"I will." He turned back to what he was doing, and after a minute or two of standing there, feeling foolish, I left and walked back to the laundromat.

I was still waiting for the machines to stop and feeling let down by Matthew when Nick, of all people, came in. He gave me a friendly smile. "Hi, Alix, how you doing?"

I'd rather have died than let him know how I was really doing, so I said, as friendly and casually as I could, "I'm okay. And you?"

"Couldn't be better. What are you doing with yourself these days?"

"Nothing much. There's not much to do."

He grinned. "I manage to keep pretty busy. Say, I'm glad I ran into you. Do you think your father would mind if I brought Mary Jane over to meet him? I'd like him to see some of her pictures. She's a heck of a good artist."

My stomach turned over. So that's why he was so friendly. "Why don't you ask him?"

"I never see him," Nick said.

"There are telephones, you know. You could call him."

He was embarrassed. "Yeah, I could. I just thought since I bumped into you, you could ask him. I don't like to bother him."

"All right," I said reluctantly.

"That would be terrific. Will you call me and let me know when it would be convenient for him?"

I gave him a look that went right past him. "Call me in a day or two."

"Sure, okay. Thanks a lot."

When he left I felt stupid. I shouldn't have said yes. Why should I help Nick help his girlfriend? It was the dumbest twist I could imagine. I felt like a sap. Twice in fifteen minutes I'd made a fool of myself. First with Matthew and now with Nick. There couldn't be two boys more different than the two of them, and I'd blown it with both of them. I'd be better off staying home locked up in my room. I couldn't do much worse.

I intended to speak to my father that night at dinner, but soon after we sat down to eat, there was a loud knock on the door. My mother was in the process of mixing a salad while my father was carving a leg of lamb, so I ran to the door. Mrs. O'Carney was there, looking agitated.

"I'm sorry to bother you," she said, "but I don't know what to do. Joe went down to the village about an hour ago to get a pack of cigarettes, and he's not back yet. My car is being serviced so I have no wheels. I'm worried something happened to him. I was wondering if one of you would mind driving me to see if I can find him."

"Come on in, I'll call my parents." She stepped inside. She was wearing a pair of tight jeans and high heels, but no makeup, and her blond hair was loose around her shoulders. She looked like a kid.

My father came in from the dining room with my mother following. Mrs. O'Carney repeated what she'd said to me.

"He probably met someone and is perfectly all right," my mother said. "If anything had happened to him you would have heard."

"I suppose," she said, but she turned her worried face from one of them to the other. I wondered if she was upset because they'd had another fight and he had gone off angry.

"But I'll be glad to take you to the village if it will make you feel better," my father offered.

She gave him a grateful smile. "I'd be very much obliged."

"I'll keep your dinner for you," my mother said.

"Oh, you were just eating. I'm so sorry . . . do you want to finish your dinner?"

"No, I can eat later," my father said. Mrs. O'Carney was visibly relieved.

My mother and I watched them go before we went back to the dining room. "She's probably all upset over nothing." My mother put some lamb, rice, and salad on a plate for me. "She seems like the type who gets hysterical easily."

"She looked really worried," I said.

Although neither of us said anything, we were both nervously waiting for my father to come home and so ate quickly. When we finished, there was still no sign of him or Mrs. O'Carney. "He could at least telephone," my mother said with a note of irritation.

It was almost an hour before they came back. Mrs. O'Carney was very distraught. "No sign of him. I can't imagine where he could be. Your husband was kind enough to ask me to wait here," she said to my mother. "Both the children are out, and I'd just as soon not be alone. I hope you don't mind."

"No, of course not. Can I get you something to eat? Or some coffee or tea?"

"I'd love a cup of coffee if it's not too much trouble."

My mother went to the kitchen and before long came back with a tray holding coffee and a few cookies. We were in the living room, and Mrs. O'Carney nibbled on a cookie nervously, picked up her cup from the coffee table, took a few sips, and put it down again. I noticed her hand gripped the cup as if she were hanging on to control herself.

"We stopped at the police station. They had no report of an accident, but they radioed the cars to be on the lookout for Joe's car," my father said. "We left this phone number with them."

"I'm sure he's all right," my mother said soothingly. "Maybe he went to look over his buildings."

Mrs. O'Carney shook her head. "No, he wouldn't do that. Not at night. Besides—" she stopped, still shaking her head as if she were trying to shake some thought out of her mind. She never finished what she was going to say.

We sat there uncomfortably. The phone rang once, and everyone jumped. But it was only Mom's friend Marie. I kept hoping Nick would get home and come over here to look for his mother. But what if he had Mary Jane with him? Then I felt guilty thinking about Nick and myself when something could have happened to Mr. O'Carney. I wished that Mr. O'Carney would come home. I didn't want anything to have happened to him, but I also didn't like having to sit this way with his wife.

Around ten o'clock Eileen came home from the movies, where she'd gone with a friend. We saw the car that brought her home pull into the O'Carney driveway. "I can go now," Mrs. O'Carney said.

"Maybe you'd rather stay here. Alix can go and bring Eileen over," my father suggested.

"Would you mind? I don't want to impose on you . . ."

"You're not," my mother said. It was obvious Mrs. O'Carney was in a bad state, and she was very relieved. I ran across the way to get Eileen.

She hugged her mother when she came back with me and sat close to her, half on her mother's lap. "Maybe Daddy just went for a ride or went to see Mr. Taylor," Eileen said, mentioning her father's partner.

"No, he wouldn't do that, not Fred Taylor." Mrs. O'Carney said the name with some disgust.

It was a little after eleven when the call came from the police. My father answered the phone. His face was grim when he held the phone out to Mrs. O'Carney.

"You talk to them," she said to him, although she stood up and walked over to him.

Whoever was at the other end was doing the talking. My father just nodded his head and said, "Yes, right," a few times, and then, "Yes, of course, I'll come with her," before he hung up.

"They found your husband and the car," he said. "There's been an accident."

She was clutching Eileen's hand in her own. "What kind of an accident? Tell me the truth, I need to know."

My father glanced at Eileen. "Perhaps . . ."

"No, she'll have to know sooner or later." Mrs. O'Carney drew in her breath. "We both will. What happened?"

My father led them back to the sofa. "Come sit down." He glanced uncertainly at them and at my mother and me. "I hate to be the one to have to tell you this. Your husband is dead."

She gasped, and Eileen buried her face against

her mother, hugging her with her arms around her. "That's what I was afraid of. How did it happen?" Mrs. O'Carney was looking directly at my father, bracing herself against the blow she seemed to be expecting.

"Carbon monoxide," my father said quietly. "He parked the car on a side road. It's a painless death."

She let out a deep sigh. "Poor Joe. Poor darling Joe." She was fighting back tears and cradling Eileen's head in her arms. "He was a good man. A remarkable man, but he was a gambler and he lost."

"Here, take some of this." My mother had poured brandy into a glass and handed it to Mrs. O'Carney. My mother looked in a daze, frightened, as if she didn't know what to do.

"Thank you." Mrs. O'Carney sipped a little brandy. Eileen still had her face pressed against her mother, but when her mother lifted the glass, Eileen sat up. She stayed close to her, her hand holding on to her mother's free arm.

"Mom, should I call Nick?" she asked in a soft voice.

"Where can you call him?"

"He may be at Mary Jane's. I can try there."

"All right, if you want to." She cupped her hands around Eileen's face. "Everything's going to be all right," she whispered. "We'll be all right."

Eileen burst into sobs and buried her face in her mother's lap. But in a few minutes she got control of herself, and I took her to the phone and watched her dial. I could hear the phone ringing, but there was no answer.

"No one's there," I said to Eileen softly. She didn't seem able to hang up.

"The police want us to come there, don't they?" she asked my father.

"Yes. They need an identification."

"Yes, of course." Mrs. O'Carney stood up. I thought again how young she looked without her makeup. In her high heels and skintight pants she looked frail, but her face was composed. "I'll need to ask you to take us there. I'm so sorry."

"Don't be silly. Of course, I'll take you," my father said.

"Eileen, you wait here," she said to her daughter.

"I want to go with you." The girl clung to her mother.

Mrs. O'Carney hesitated a moment. "All right, if that's what you want. Are you sure you want to come? It's not going to be pleasant, honey."

"I'm sure. I'll be okay." She held her mother's hand as they left. My mother and I stood at the door and watched them go.

"That poor woman," my mother said. "I feel

so sorry for her." She shook her head sadly. "I don't know how she's going to manage without him. She doesn't seem like someone who can take care of herself and those children. I think she was very dependent on him."

"I think they were all dependent on him. He was kind of the moving force in the family. I wonder why he did it."

"You heard what she said. He gambled and lost. I do hope she'll be left all right financially. They seem to need a great deal of money for their life-style."

"I know," I agreed.

My mother and I were both nervous and oddly uncomfortable with each other while we waited for my father to come home. We fussed around in the kitchen and then sat out in back looking at the stars. It was a glorious night, a terrible night to die in, I thought. I had never seen anyone dead, but I had an image in my mind of Mr. O'Carney slumped in his car seat. It was hard to imagine that healthy-looking, handsome man not telling everyone what to do.

Every once in a while my mother glanced over at me, and I wondered if we were both thinking the same thing: We should have been nicer to the O'Carneys. Not that any of us did anything bad to them, but we had looked down on them and made fun of them to ourselves, when all the time they may have been having a terrible time. If we had been nicer, better neighbors, would it have made any difference? I wanted to die with shame when I thought of the first time Mr. O'Carney had come to introduce himself and brought the lilacs. If he had become friends with my father, had had him to talk to, maybe he wouldn't have driven down that country road tonight to do what he did.

I felt very frightened. It suddenly struck me that no one ever really knows another person, even someone close. I didn't know what went on inside my own mother, she didn't know my thoughts, what I feared, what I dreamt of. It was a cold, dark thought, and I reached out my hand and took hold of my mother's. She held mine tight in hers, and I felt a warm surge of relief. Maybe after all, people didn't have to know each other's thoughts, maybe it was enough just knowing there was someone there who loved you and whom you loved back.

When my father came home, he sank down on his big chair exhausted. He looked awful. My mother gave him a glass of brandy, which he drank in a few gulps.

"It must have been a terrible experience for that poor woman. And for the child. She never should have gone." My mother was shaking her head sadly. "And for you, too, my poor darling. Did they carry on badly?"

My father had a strange, pained look in his eyes when he answered. "No, they didn't carry on. They were terrific, the two of them. I think they impressed everyone—the cops, the doctor. That woman has a lot of guts, so does the kid. She can put us all to shame, Constance."

"She is in a state of shock," my mother said. "I worry about what she will do when she comes to and realizes what has happened. I'm afraid she doesn't have much inner strength to fall back on."

"We'll see," my father said, and his eyes still looked as if he were hurting somewhere.

I left my parents and went up to my room. I needed to think. I thought about Nick and his hearing this terrible news, wishing there was something I could do to help him. It was hard to connect him or his family with tragedy; they had all seemed so blithe about their lives. I couldn't imagine Nick being sad.

Ten

I DIDN'T SEE NICK UNTIL THE NEXT DAY. THERE were several cars and a great deal of activity across the road all morning, but after lunch my parents and I went to the O'Carney house. Mrs. O'Carney greeted us at the door. Her face was pale and strained; but she looked cool and neat in a simple black cotton shift, her hair caught up on top of her head with a narrow black-velvet ribbon. She was bare-legged and wearing her inevitable high heels. She looked slightly startled when my mother put her arms around her and kissed her.

"Are you all right?" My mother scanned her face anxiously.

"I guess so. Yes, I'm all right. Come in, please."

The living room was filled with people. Nick

and Eileen were there, and I recognized Mr. O'Carney's parents, and an older version of Dyan O'Carney—more lines, more bleach, thicker body—who had to be her mother. I greeted Eileen and kissed her, and she gave me a warm hug.

Nick came over to us when we walked in, shook hands with my father, kissed my mother on the cheek—to her surprise—and gave me a fraternal hug. I looked around to see if Mary Jane was there, but she wasn't. I wondered why, until I remembered that Eileen said Mrs. O'Carney didn't like her.

I suppose we did what people do on occasions like that. We tried to make rather inane conversation—weather, gardens, the weather again. The elder Mrs. O'Carney was the one who first mentioned his name. She said something like, "Joe was a wonderful boy, a wonderful son, a good father . . . how could he do such a thing?" Then she sobbed for a bit until her husband quieted her down, holding her and whispering to her quietly. Somehow her open grief put people more at ease, as though everyone remembered why they were there and that it was all right to talk about Mr. O'Carney and to feel badly.

As people began to talk about him, I wondered how Mrs. O'Carney, Nick, and Eileen felt. Eileen stayed very quiet with a subdued look on her face, but Nick joined in, telling some anecdotes about his father. Mrs. O'Carney moved nervously around the room and laughed a little at one amusing story about her husband. She insisted on being the hostess, refilling the coffeepot, taking empty cups and saucers to the kitchen and coming back with clean ones. She wouldn't let anyone help her, saying that she needed to be busy.

I felt peculiar about Nick; he had such a worried, unhappy look on his face. I wished we had gotten close so that I could try to comfort him now. It was awful to be so aware of his presence in a tragic situation like this and yet not to be able to do anything about it. I wanted to put my arms around him; but, knowing about Mary Jane, I didn't even know how to talk to him. When he went into the hall a couple of times to use the phone, I was sure he was calling her.

We didn't stay very long. After we got home, we all went into the backyard. My mother and I were sitting on chaises longues, while my father walked about breaking dead twigs off our trees. Then he stopped and stretched out on a lawn chair, too.

"Dyan O'Carney's asked us to come to a small service for her husband tomorrow at the funeral home. She's having him cremated," he said, "and since she doesn't belong to a church here, she thought that would be the best. She wanted to do something. I wonder what's going to happen to her."

"What do you mean?" my mother asked.

"I suspect he must have lost a lot of money. Probably all they had."

"That would be awful." My mother was shocked. "They're so dependent on their possessions, I'd hate to think of her being poor."

"I know," my father agreed. "That's the trouble with wanting to buy everything that comes along. But Joe O'Carney seemed like such a successful man, it's hard to understand. Just shows how little one knows people."

"We did know they weren't very substantial," my mother said.

"You didn't know any such thing," I flared up. "You never bothered to get to know them. You judged them by how they dressed, by their house and furniture. You two made up your minds about them for the most superficial reasons. Because they have different taste from yours, you decided they were no good. I don't think you have to put down people with different tastes nor feel superior about your own. They probably get as much pleasure out of what you consider ugly as you do from your beautiful antiques. I think it was horrid that we laughed at Mrs. O'Carney's furniture. I'm ashamed of it, if you're not. You have no right to talk that way about them now."

"Alix, darling," my father said, "poor Mr. O'Carney's suicide only proves, unfortunately, what we've been saying. They are flimsy people who got into debt to buy all that stuff they have. They put material things above everything else."

"That's not fair," I cried. "Mr. O'Carney got into debt in business, you said that yourself."

At this point my mother interrupted with a sigh. "Let's not talk about the O'Carneys anymore. It's foolish for us to get into an argument over them."

Although I wanted them to admit that they were wrong, I dropped the conversation, too.

I hated going to the funeral parlor. I'd never been inside one before, although I had passed this one a million times. It was a large white building on Main Street, with a beautiful lawn and flower borders, that had once been someone's mansion. Although the inside was rather elegantly furnished, the dark wood on the walls and the dark furniture were depressing, and the place seemed to smell of death. Everyone spoke in whispers.

The same people who had been at the house the day before, plus a few more who were probably business friends of Mr. O'Carney's, were gathered in a somber room. A young minister whom we didn't know conducted a brief service. Mrs. O'Carney sat with Nick and Eileen on either side of her and only broke down momentarily, when her mother-in-law gave way to sobs. The whole thing was over in about twenty minutes. On leaving, Mrs. O'Carney asked us to come back to the house for refreshments.

Something had happened to Nick overnight. At their house that afternoon, he seemed to take charge. He brought chairs into the living room for people to sit on, he asked his grandfather to make drinks, he told Eileen to bring the coffee-pot from the kitchen. He was very solicitous of his mother, insisting that she sit down in a comfortable chair and assuring her that he and Eileen could take care of everything.

It seemed he had suddenly grown up. It was hard to connect this boy, who even seemed to hold himself straighter, with the careless, slouchy kid whose biggest thrill a short while back was setting off firecrackers.

As I sat there, watching him act the head of the family, I did some heavy thinking about myself. It would have been nice to feel that I had been attracted to Nick because I had known all along there was depth behind his outward superficiality, but it just wasn't true. I knew nothing of the sort. The attraction, besides the strong physical pull, had been my own need to break out of a mold. Now that I was seeing a new side to Nick, I felt ashamed. I realized that I got what I deserved: My feelings were one-sided because I had only been thinking of myself. I needed Nick, I wanted something from him, but I sure didn't give much thought to what I could give to him. I had even hated the idea of being a good influence. No wonder I lost out.

I winced when I thought about how happy he and Mary Jane seemed that day at McDonald's, and the loving way she had looked at him. The infatuation I had for Nick had so many questions, so many holes, so many things I was afraid of. Mary Jane had looked at him with a trust that I had never felt. She *cared* about him, she really cared, and obviously he returned the feeling because it was real. Oh boy, with all my education I was the one who had a heck of a lot to learn about feelings.

I sat near the window a little way off from the rest of the people, not paying attention to the general conversation. I was so involved thinking about Nick and myself that when he came over to me I was taken aback. What if he had been reading my mind? He sat down on the window seat next to me.

"How are you doing?" I asked him softly.

"Okay, I guess. I hope Eileen will be all right. It's going to be hard on her. She really adored my father. She was his baby girl."

"It's lousy for all three of you. But your mother's been fantastic. My mother thinks it really hasn't hit her yet."

Nick nodded. "Yeah, I know. But she's going to be okay. She's a terrific person. She hasn't had an easy time of it, but she's very gutsy."

We were both speaking quietly, behind the noise of the people in the room talking. After a few minutes Nick spoke again. "She loved my father, but she went through plenty with him." He looked at me and his eyes were sad. "He shouldn't have done this to her, but it was typical. He could never face responsibility, and this was his way of ducking out, not facing the financial mess." There was a tinge of anger in his voice. "You're probably shocked to hear me talk this way. I loved my father, too, but he shouldn't have done this, never." He shook his head despairingly.

"I'm sorry." I touched his arm. I felt close to him then, but in a different way—friendly, not mind-blowing.

"Alix, would you do me a favor?" Nick turned to face me.

"Sure, if I can."

"I hope you won't mind my asking you this. I

was supposed to pick up Mary Jane after work tonight. I thought I could get away, but my grandparents and some other people are staying, so I'd better stay here. She's not supposed to get phone calls at work, so I was wondering if you could stop around at the restaurant and give her a message for me?"

I was stunned. But, of course, Nick didn't know how I had felt about him. It was all in my own head. "Where's the restaurant?" I asked in a remarkably composed voice.

"In the village. You'd have to ride your bike . . ."

"I'd have to go before it got dark."

"You could go any time, she's there from two o'clock on."

"Well, sure." I glanced at my watch, and saw it was almost two o'clock. "I could go now." I wanted to get this weird errand over with, so I wouldn't have to think about it all day. "What do you want me to tell her?"

"I'll write a note." He gave me a warm smile. "It's terrific of you to do this. I really appreciate it."

"Forget it."

He left but came back in a few minutes and handed me an envelope.

After saying good-bye to Mrs. O'Carney and

telling my parents that I had to return a book to the library that was due that day, I left. I couldn't believe what I was doing. Yet everything that had happened over the past two days was so strange, this wasn't any more so. Besides, I was glad I was able to be doing something for Nick, even a small thing like this.

The Corner Cafe where Mary Jane worked was a small coffee shop off Main Street. It was in a nondescript building and had plate glass windows advertising a full breakfast for 99¢ and hot specials for $2.39. I had never been inside it in all the years I'd lived in Mill Pond.

The inside was more appealing than the outside—with tables, booths, and a long, pale wood counter. It was after lunch and the place was almost empty. Mary Jane was behind the counter. She saw me immediately, and her face looked alarmed. "What brings you here?" she asked with a nervous smile.

I sat down on a stool opposite her, suddenly tired. I had biked there quickly, and my legs ached. "Just a message from Nick." I pulled his note out of my pocket and handed it to her.

"Is he all right?" she asked before opening it.

"Yes, he's fine. That is, you know, pretty good—it's been rough. He wanted to come here himself but he couldn't get away. All the relatives are at the house, millions of people."

She nodded. I watched her while she read his note. The happy smile that crossed her face gave me a pang of jealousy. I wished I had been the one Nick loved. The pain of my failure hit me anew. I saw myself as the dumb go-between, carrying messages for them. What a dope I was.

Mary Jane tucked the note into her apron pocket. "Just tell him it's all right," she said with a wide smile. "Tell him not to worry, I understand."

"Do you want to send him back a note?" I asked.

"No, I don't need to. How are his mother and sister?"

"They're okay, I guess."

"Do you want a cup of coffee?"

"I didn't bring any money with me."

"You don't need any. Here." She poured a cup for me, and brought over the sugar bowl and milk.

"Thanks." The hot coffee felt good.

"It's awful what happened." Mary Jane leaned against the counter. "I can't imagine anyone doing such a thing. I'm so afraid they're going to move away now."

"Why should they move away?"

She looked at me with surprise and, I thought, a little pity. "Money, of course. I think he lost it all. You wouldn't understand. You can't live in a big house like that if you don't have any money. They'll probably lose the house."

"That would be terrible." I met her eyes, and as her words sank in, I felt some anger. "Why do you say I wouldn't understand? I'm not a baby, I know about money."

"Nick said you were overprotected. I wouldn't know, but I did have the feeling you were kind of wrapped in cotton. Or maybe I should say silk," she added cleverly.

"If I am it's not my fault," I said defensively. "My parents brought me up that way."

She stood back with her arms folded and looked at me with narrowed eyes. She wasn't gorgeous, but I could see why boys would fall for her. She was provocative with a challenging air that said, I can take care of myself. "Listen," she said, "my parents didn't bring me up at all. They haven't even been around. It's what *you* do that counts. Kids like you blame everything on your parents. Baloney. You're all spoiled. You've got eyes and ears and a brain. What you are is up to you."

I didn't know what to say and just stared at her. She wasn't meek and soft the way she'd been when I'd met her with Nick. I was impressed—I was facing someone who knew who she was. But she also knew how to be with a boy, to be loving yet still be independent. I had to hand it to her.

"Look at me," she went on, as if my angry remark had triggered something deep inside her. "I didn't even finish high school, but I'm not going to be working behind this counter all my life. I'm saving my money, and I'm going to art school. I made up my mind. I'm going to be a designer. Wallpaper, fabric. You ask Nick, he's seen the stuff I do. He wanted me to show it to your father, but it's not his kind of painting. It's not fine art, it's designs, I know enough to know that. I got a lot to learn but I'll learn it—you'll see."

"You can still show it to my father," I said. "Maybe he could help you." I'm not sure why I suggested that, I was still jealous of her and Nick. But as she talked, I found myself admiring her, too. She knew what she wanted, where she was going—she made me feel so childish. Granted, she was three or four years older than I was, but I wondered if I would know as much as she did when I was her age.

"I don't like to bother anyone," she said.

"It's up to you."

I finished my coffee and got up. "Guess I'd better go. Thanks for the coffee. Anything else you want me to tell Nick?"

"Just what I said. And give him my love," she added with an unexpected shy smile.

I biked home more slowly. I didn't feel like going back to the O'Carneys, especially after what Mary Jane just told me. If they were really going to lose their house, then what good did all Mr. O'Carney's possessions do him now? And if they did lose everything, would Nick, Eileen, and their mother be able to bear it? Did their happiness in life depend on material things?

When I got home, I telephoned Nick and gave him the message from Mary Jane. After thanking me, he asked, "How is she? Is she okay?"

"Yes, she seemed fine. She sends her love," I added.

"Thanks. Thanks a lot, Alix, you're a good friend."

After I hung up the phone, I sat and stared out the window. I felt lonely and confused. I went into the living room and put a Brahms sonata on the stereo. I turned it down to a soft, low tone and sat listening and thinking. Mary Jane had called me a spoiled child. Was that a truer word than special? It probably was. I thought about all the advantages I had been given and how I was blaming my parents for giving them to me. As if it was their fault that I was such a jerk. Mary Jane knew where she wanted to go—like Matthew did. Although they were worlds apart, Mary Jane and Matthew both stood on their own, and they both made me feel like a wimp. Even crazy Nick was suddenly a responsible person. If he could change, couldn't I?

Eleven

FOR SEVERAL DAYS AFTER THE FUNERAL WE
saw the O'Carneys only briefly, but at the
end of the week Mrs. O'Carney phoned and
asked if she could come over. It was around four
o'clock on a hot afternoon and my parents and I
were sitting outside drinking iced tea. Of course
they told her to come and join us out back.

A few minutes later she appeared. My father
pulled over a chair and faced it so that the sun
would not be in her eyes. She lay back for a few
minutes as if this were the first time she'd sat down
all week. She looked very tired. Her face seemed
thinner and there were dark circles around her
eyes.

"It's nice to sit here," she said. She had a wistful, poignant expression as she looked at all three of us. "It's very serene."

"You must have been having a rough time," my mother said. "Is your mother still with you?"

"No, she's gone home to New Jersey. My father's not well. That's why he didn't come with her. I came over to tell you that we'll be leaving soon. We're going to stay with my folks for a while. They have a big house, and it seems like the best thing to do."

"We're sorry to hear that," my father said. "Are you selling the house?"

Mrs. O'Carney shook her head. With a wry smile she said, "I wish we were. It's not ours to sell. Joe didn't pay the mortgage for months. The bank owns the house, not us."

"But that's terrible." My mother looked at her with distress. "Won't you get anything for it?"

"I'm afraid not. To tell you the truth, we'll be leaving here with our clothes—that's about all. That and some debts. We owe on everything." She spoke calmly.

"But what will you do? It's fine that you have your parents to go to, but to lose everything . . ." My mother was fumbling for words. "Your furniture, all the things you have, it's going to be hard for you and the children. All of you seemed to get so much pleasure out of the cars, the motorcycle, the games. . . . Can't you save any of it?"

"No, we can't," Mrs. O'Carney said flatly. Then she gave my mother a disarming smile. "All those things aren't as important to us as you may think. Sure we enjoyed them, they were fun, but that's all they were—fun. We're a very close family, and we can get along on very little, too. That's what poor Joe didn't understand, that we didn't *need* those things. He wanted to provide them, he needed them to feel important. That was his tragedy. Joe couldn't do anything small—he couldn't build one house, he had to build ten houses. He gambled big and he lost big." She lay back in her chair and closed her eyes for a few minutes. "Joe couldn't help what he did, it was just the way he was."

We all sat quietly for several minutes until my father broke the silence. "You're a brave lady. I admire you."

Mrs. O'Carney laughed. "I'm not brave at all. I can't put all the blame on Joe. If I had been stronger I might have stopped him, but I let him handle everything. Now I have to be practical. We'll be all right, though. I have two wonderful kids, and I'll get some kind of a job. I don't know about Nick. I'd like to see him go to college, and maybe he will in a year or two. He's going to get a job, my father has something lined up for him at home." Then she turned to me. "Nick said you don't own a television set, and I thought you might like to have ours. It's the one thing we don't owe on, and my folks have two in their house. Unless there's some reason you don't want it?" She looked at my parents questioningly.

My mother seemed uncomfortable. "Actually, we don't have one because we didn't think it necessary. We have a lot of music in the house, and Alix gets to see plenty of entertainment. It's very kind of you, but . . ."

"I don't want to make a problem for you." Mrs. O'Carney spoke cautiously. "You probably think there's nothing but trash on the tube, but there are good things, too. Besides," she added with a shy grin, "some of the silly shows can be relaxing. Of course I'm not as sophisticated as you are, but a good laugh doesn't hurt."

"Mom, please. Please let me have it, please." I was terribly moved by Mrs. O'Carney's offer. Not only to have the TV, but because she wanted to give it to me.

My parents were looking at each other. "It's a very generous offer," my father said. "Wouldn't it be better if you sold it? You could probably get quite a bit of money for it."

"I doubt it. None of these expensive toys are worth much secondhand. But even so I'd like Alix to have it. We all would. It's been nice having people like you for neighbors."

My mother's face turned crimson. "You're being much too kind. We haven't been very good neighbors, I'm afraid," she murmured.

"But you have. Just knowing you and knowing you were here gave me a feeling of security. It's always good to know people who live differently from the way you yourself do. I like that."

Soon afterward Mrs. O'Carney got up to leave. I nudged my mother. "What about the television?" I whispered.

Mrs. O'Carney heard me and laughed. "Yes, what about it? Can Nick bring it over?"

My parents exchanged glances again, and my father looked at me. "You really want it, don't you?"

I nodded my head. "Yes, I do."

"It's a very generous present. But if you really want to give it to her . . ."

"Oh, Dad, thank you, thank you." I threw my arms around him, and then I hugged Mrs. O'Carney. "I don't know how to thank you. It's the most fabulous present I've ever received. I'll think of you every time I turn it on."

"I hope that won't be too often," my mother said with a smile.

After Mrs. O'Carney left I felt excited about the TV, but then sad because I was only getting it because they were leaving. "Isn't it awful that just when we've gotten to know the O'Carneys better they're leaving? And it took Mr. O'Carney's dying for us to see what a terrific family they are," I said to my mother and father. The three of us were still sitting outside, watching the sun fall behind the trees.

"She'll be better off near a big city," my mother said. "I don't think she'd be happy here. And I doubt we'd ever be close friends."

"Why do you say that?"

"Because even though Dyan O'Carney may be a good person, we really have little in common. Our interests aren't the same. And, besides, I still think she has atrocious taste. I admit I was too quick to judge her, but that doesn't change her. I don't claim to be a superior person, but I am different from her. She may be stronger than I gave her credit for being, but she doesn't have to be my bosom friend."

"Well, *I'm* glad we had the O'Carneys as

neighbors and that I got to know them," I said matter-of-factly.

We sat quietly for a little while. Then my mother said, "I guess I should go in to start dinner. Unless"—she turned to me with a mischievous look—"you want to go to McDonald's."

I laughed with her. "I don't want to make a habit of it. I still like your cooking."

"Thank you," my mother said, and gave me a kiss.

I was surprised to get a call from Nick a few days after Mrs. O'Carney's visit. He asked if I had time to ride with him into the village to get a soda or some ice cream. It was a hot afternoon, and I was just sitting around being lazy.

"Yeah, sure," I told him, wondering what he wanted.

It wasn't until we got to the ice-cream parlor and were sitting down with large sundaes that I found out. "You know we're leaving for New Jersey in about a week or so," he said. "My mother wants to get out as fast as she can. I have a funny favor to ask you. I know you're kind of a loner, but I wonder if after I go, you'd stop in to see Mary Jane once in a while, or call her up." He must have seen the astonishment on my face, so he went on hurriedly. "I know it's a peculiar thing to ask you, but she's a terrific girl. She's not at all what you think or what people say about her. That's the trouble—people aren't very nice to her and so she's always on the defensive. I know she's older than you are, but I think if you two got to know each other you'd hit it off. She's deep and so are you. And she's got terrific talent. Maybe you can persuade her to show her things to your father." His eyes were looking directly into mine. "I hate leaving her."

I was completely taken by surprise. "She'd think I'm an awful kid," I said lamely. I really didn't know what to say.

"No, she likes you, she said so."

"She doesn't even know me."

"She thought it was very nice that you brought her my note." He leaned toward me. "Even if you don't get to be buddy-buddy friends, it would be terrific if you would just keep in touch with her. Mary Jane was very impressed when she met you. She's big on culture and eager to learn. Having someone like you bothering to see her would give her confidence. Honestly, don't laugh. You may not realize it, but you're really someone special."

Then I had to laugh. Nick had no idea what he had said to me. Someone special. For the first time in my life it sounded good, and I flushed with the compliment.

"You're blushing," Nick said, and he laughed with me. "You *will* do it, won't you?"

"Sure, of course, I will."

We went on to talk about other things—his moving away, his job in his grandfather's printing business—and it felt like talking to an old friend.

When Nick drove me home we didn't say good-bye. "We'll see each other before we go," he said.

"Yeah, sure," I agreed. I felt empty when I left him.

Twelve

ALL WEEK LONG WE WATCHED AS FURNITURE and appliances were moved out of the O'Carney house—the large sofa, a huge freezer, tools, the snow-blower—everything we had watched get moved in. "I don't see how she can bear it," my mother said.

But when we saw Mrs. O'Carney outside, directing the truck drivers, she seemed composed and cheerful. The house was totally empty when my parents and I went over to say good-bye. The O'Carneys were leaving the next day.

"I can't even offer you a seat," Mrs. O'Carney said with a laugh. "There aren't any chairs."

"That's all right," my mother said. "We won't stay anyway. We just came to say good-bye." She kissed Mrs. O'Carney. "And to wish you the best of everything."

I had a strange feeling as we chatted together. Even though my parents would never agree with me, I felt that we had missed a chance at something. The O'Carneys were leaving just when we were getting to know them and to discover how much was beneath the superficial surface. I wished they were just moving in and we could start all over again. I had gotten a lot from them—more than they had from me and I was sorry to see them go.

Before we left Nick said he would bring the TV set over later. "And you won't forget about Mary Jane, will you?" he asked in a low voice.

"No, I won't forget. But I still don't know what makes you think she'd want to be friends with me."

"Take my word for it. I know she'd like to hear from you."

I hate good-byes, so the next day when they finally left I ran outside, kissed them, and went back into the house. But I couldn't resist seeing them actually go, so I watched from the window as they drove off in Mrs. O'Carney's car.

My parents stayed outside until the O'Carneys were out of sight. When they came back in, our big discussion was where to put the TV. My mother didn't want it in the living room, so I suggested putting it in my room. "If you two don't want to watch it, that's the best place," I said.

I laughed at my father when he objected. "We may want to watch it sometime," he said, without looking at my mother.

"You're weakening, Dad."

He shrugged. "Since it's in the house, there may be something worthwhile that we'd all want to see." He had a childish smile on his face.

We finally decided to put the set in a small room downstairs that had once been known as a morning room and was now somewhat of a junk room. I offered to clean it up so there would be room for the big TV set and for a small couch and a couple of chairs.

I noticed my mother came in a few times to look at it.

"I hope you'll enjoy this," I said.

"I have an open mind. I'll give it a try." She had an impish smile as she turned the knobs, but since we didn't have the antenna up yet, we couldn't get a picture.

With the excitement of finally having our own TV to watch, I didn't think about my promise to

Nick for a few days. When I finally thought about Mary Jane, I knew I didn't at all feel like going to see her, but I had promised. So about a week after the O'Carneys left, I rode my bike into the village.

She was behind the counter at the restaurant, just as she had been before. I climbed on to one of the stools opposite her. We both said hi and again she offered me a cup of coffee, but I took a glass of orange juice instead. I really didn't know what to say to her.

"How are you doing?" I asked.

"Okay. I miss Nick. Have you heard from him?"

"No, I didn't expect to. Have you?"

"Yes, sure. He's called me a few times. He doesn't really like living in his grandmother's house. Says she fusses too much. When he has enough money, he's going to get himself an apartment."

"That'll be nice." I was wondering if she was planning to go to live with him, but I didn't have the nerve to ask. I didn't have to.

"He wants me to come down there," she said. "I won't go to his grandmother's, but maybe when he has his own place, I might go for a visit. But that's all," she added. "I'm not giving up on art school. Someday I'll get there."

"Why don't you come over and show some of your work to my father?" I asked impulsively. "Maybe he can help you."

"What could he do for me?" She was very direct.

"I don't know, but he knows a lot of people in the art world. He knows people who teach. Maybe he could help get you into an art school."

"I don't like to ask for favors," she said. "Your father doesn't even know me, why should he want to bother?"

"Please come over. If he can't, he can't, but we can at least try." Suddenly I found it terribly important to help her. I didn't want to be patronizing, but I felt that I, that we—my parents and I—were being put on the line. Here was someone serious about being creative, and if what my father had said to me about protecting the arts was true, we should do something about it. "When can you come?"

"Tomorrow's my day off," she said hesitatingly. "Do you really think I should?"

"Definitely. Come over after lunch, around two. Is that okay?"

She gave me her shy smile. "Okay, if you say so."

"I say so."

I was peculiarly excited about Mary Jane coming over. My father had merely shrugged when I'd told him and said he didn't know what he could do for her and that he hoped that neither she nor he would be embarrassed. "I hate to do this, because if her work's no good, I'm on the spot. I wish you had asked me first."

"I'm sorry, but I had to ask her then. I felt it was important. Maybe she'll surprise you."

"I doubt it, but it's too late now."

I couldn't explain to him or to my mother why I felt this was important. They'd think I was trying to play fairy godmother, but it wasn't that at all. It was in a funny way connected with my feeling for Nick. As if this proved that falling for him hadn't been a waste, that I had gotten something important from him. Not the TV, which was nice, but understanding about him and Mary Jane, that they were worthwhile people with whom I could really be friends. After all, I had been too quick to judge her, doing exactly what I had accused my parents of doing with the O'Carneys.

Mary Jane appeared promptly at two o'clock the next afternoon. She drove up in a battered old car, but she had dressed carefully in a white cotton skirt and a navy jersey top. She carried a large portfolio under her arm. I met her outside and led her around the back to my father's studio.

My father greeted her cordially. Her eyes looked around the studio with the same wonder and admiration that Nick's had. "What a wonderful place to work in," she said. "It's beautiful."

My father cleared space on a table, and Mary Jane opened her folio for him. While I watched my father's face as he turned over one sheet after another, I felt my body tense up. Every part of me was concentrating on wanting him to like her work. It could have been something of my own he was looking at, I was wishing so hard for his approval.

I couldn't tell anything from his face. He stopped several times to study a drawing more carefully. I was afraid to look at Mary Jane. She stood with her arms folded across her chest as if holding herself in.

There were quite a few drawings and paintings. After my father looked at them once, he went back and looked at some of them again. Was that a good sign? Finally he closed the portfolio and turned to Mary Jane.

"You have talent," he said, and I sighed with relief. "You have a good sense of color and design; but, of course, as I am sure you know, you have a lot to learn. You let your paints get muddy when they should be clear and bright. If you want to make a living at this, I would suggest you study design. Textile design. Very few artists make a living at fine painting, and I couldn't encourage you along that line."

"But design is what I want. It's what I like to do," Mary Jane said. "I'm saving my money for school. Which do you think I should try for?" Her face was eager.

"There are several good schools. Rhode Island School of Design is one, and there are others. When you are ready, I can give you the names of a few you could write to."

"That would be wonderful. I don't know how to thank you. You were terrific to take the time to look at my things. Do you really think I could do it?" She looked at my father as if he were able to wave a magic wand.

"With a lot of hard work. There's never a guarantee. You'll see when you go to school the competition is tough. There is a lot of talent around, and some get there and some don't. Connections help when it comes to a job, but I don't suppose you have any."

"Not a soul. I don't know anybody."

"All you can do is try. I wish you luck. You're picking a hard career for yourself, but if it's what you want it's worth a try."

Mary Jane admired his sculpture, and after a

148

little while she left. My father came back to the house with me for his afternoon cup of tea, and we sat outside with my mother.

"So, what do you think?" I asked him. "Is she really good?"

"I told her the truth. She has a sense of color and design, but she needs to learn her craft. I doubt she'll stick with it, though. You have to really be committed. I suspect she'll remain a waitress or get married."

"You have no right to say that," I said indignantly. "She's only working as a waitress so she can save money to go to school. She'll get there, you'll see."

"There's nothing in her background that would make her do that," my mother said. "Your father's probably right." She poured tea for the three of us.

"I don't understand you two, you're doing it again." I was yelling at them. "What's her background got to do with it? She's a person, she's been taking care of herself for years already. I think you should help her, Dad."

"Me? What can I do to help her? And why should I? I hardly know her." My father picked up his cup and looked at me with amused eyes.

"Because you're supposed to believe in art. Only

a few weeks ago you told me that society needs people like you, like us. What good is it if you can't help someone like Mary Jane?"

"That's not what I meant," my father said. "Society needs artists, writers, musicians because of what they contribute to the quality of life, to the general culture. We'd have a barren world without them. It's not a question of helping an individual."

"Why isn't it? It seems to me it's part of the same thing. You're just dealing in abstract terms. Now when there's a chance to be specific, to put your philosophy to work, you don't want to do it. That's phony." I was furious now.

My father sat up straight and looked at me sternly. "You have no right to say that to me. I am not a phony just because I don't agree with you. I am not at all sure I can help this new friend of yours; but if I do, it would only be because she seems to be someone you want to help. The Mary Janes are not great artists who will make beautiful and important contributions to the world."

"Who cares if it's important? And who are you to decide what's beautiful? That is where you and I differ. Not everything has to be great art or be important to give people pleasure. The O'Carneys' house was ugly to you, but they liked it. Mary

Jane's designs may give a lot of people pleasure without being 'great art.' " I was as determined as he. "Will you help her?"

"What do you think he can do?" my mother asked. She had been listening to us with a nervous expression on her face. She was used to our discussions, but not to my father and me getting angry.

"Dad knows people. Maybe he could help her get a scholarship to one of the schools he knows about."

"That's not easy," my father said. "I do know J.B. Allen in New York, he's on the board of a good school. I suppose I could write to him . . ." He was looking at me thoughtfully. "But I know so little about her. I hate to recommend someone who might drop out after a few months."

"She won't. Give her the benefit of the doubt. You said she had talent, give her a chance. What if she did drop out? It wouldn't do anything to you."

"Maybe not directly, but it wouldn't look good. It's a risk."

"Oh, Dad, for heaven's sake. So take a risk. What if she turned out to be terrific? That could happen, too." I shook my head despairingly. "Just help someone. It would mean so much to her."

And to me, too, I thought. I needed them to make a commitment that I could understand. That wasn't just talk. That was real.

I couldn't quite read the expression in my father's eyes when he looked at me. Was there a hint of admiration, of wonder, of amusement? At least he wasn't angry anymore. "Okay, I'll write to Allen. If she did get a scholarship, would she be ready to go in the fall?"

"Absolutely. I know she would. She'd go in a minute."

"Don't say anything to her until I hear from him. There's no sense raising her hopes."

"I won't say a word." I threw my arms around my father and hugged him. "Thank you, I'm very grateful."

Thirteen

NATURALLY I COULDN'T WAIT UNTIL MY father heard from Mr. Allen. I was afraid to go to see Mary Jane for fear I'd say something. But I did stop in at the restaurant once so she wouldn't think I'd forgotten about her. Although she was almost nineteen, sometimes I felt that I was the older one. She was much more sophisticated than I about life, but she treated me as if I knew more. "You're smarter than me," she said to me more than once. "You know a lot, you've read more." I didn't feel smarter.

When I saw her at the restaurant she asked me if my father had said anything. "What did he really think?"

"He told you the truth. He thinks you're very talented, but you need to learn more."

"I know. School seems a long way off, though. I save so little money." She sighed.

I was dying to say something, but I didn't.

The summer was dull. Julie was away, and so I spent most of my time reading and playing the piano. The only excitement was watching the real estate agents show the O'Carney house. Some pretty weird-looking people came to look at it. After a while, we heard that a retired couple were interested in buying it. My parents liked that, but I was disappointed. They sounded boring. No children.

A few weeks after the O'Carneys had left, my mother took me by surprise. My father had already gone out to the studio, and she and I were having breakfast. "I think we should have a party," she announced.

"A party?" As long as I could remember, my parents had never had a party. "Who would you invite?"

Her face became thoughtful. "I don't know. We don't know many people, do we? I thought you might like a party. Some of your friends from school?"

I shook my head. "No, I don't know anyone I want to invite to a party."

"There must be some young people . . ." She gave me a troubled look.

"There aren't any," I said. "I don't want a party, but thank you anyway."

"What about asking that nice boy over? The one who bought your father's piece of sculpture."

"I don't think so, he probably never wants to see me again." I was sure he wouldn't, and I felt embarrassed just thinking about the last time I saw him. "But what's gotten into you anyway?" I eyed my mother suspiciously. "Suddenly worried about my social life?"

"Yes, I am. Your father and I think we haven't paid enough attention to the fact that we have a teenage daughter. Maybe we've kept you too much with us. Not that we go for rock and roll and all that sort of thing—but maybe we've pushed you too much the other way."

I laughed. "Matthew's not exactly a different way. Is this the O'Carney influence?" I asked bluntly.

"In a way, yes. We're not too old to learn a thing or two," she added lightly.

"Good for you. I'm glad. I appreciate your effort, but I think I'll find my own way. I learned a thing or two also. I am going to ask Mary Jane over sometime if she can come, though."

My mother looked a little surprised, but she bravely said, "Sure, if you want to, but she's rather older than you are."

"I know, but I think she'd like to come."

When my mother went into the kitchen, I sat at the dining room table and thought about Matthew. I wondered if he would come if I asked him over, and if I could bear taking the risk of his saying no. It was something I'd have to think about carefully.

Before I got around to asking Mary Jane to come over, my father got a phone call from Mr. Allen in New York. There was some scholarship money available, he said, and if my father knew of a worthy candidate, he would like to arrange for an interview. I was ecstatic and wanted to go immediately to tell Mary Jane.

"Take it easy," my father said. "Hold on. Before I call him back I want her to give me some information about herself. Ask her to write a page or two giving me her background, her education, her jobs. He's going to want to know all that anyway."

"But she hasn't much formal education. I don't think she even finished high school," I wailed. "And just schlocky jobs. What's that got to do with her painting?"

"She going to have to tell them about herself." My father looked stubborn.

"Then let her tell it to them herself. Why does

she have to write it for you?" I knew that would put Mary Jane off.

"I want to see how she'd do. If I'm sponsoring her, I've a right to know."

"You're being stuffy. You know her, you met her, you saw her work."

"Why are you so concerned?" my father asked.

"Because I am. All this culture I've been fed— well, now I want to help someone else. Otherwise, I feel like it's useless."

"*That* it's useless," my father corrected me sternly. Then he smiled. "All right, do-gooder, do it your way. Ask her when she can go down to see Allen."

"I'm *not* a do-gooder," I said emphatically. I hated that expression and it was not the way I thought of myself. After all it wasn't any *big* thing I was doing for Mary Jane. I liked her and what I had said to my father was true, and it was as true for them as it was for me: Here was their chance to put their homage to art to a practical use. If they didn't take it, they weren't special at all, just phonies. And I would be the same.

When I went to the restaurant and told Mary Jane she was to go for an interview, she looked scared. "What will I have to do?"

"Probably just answer some questions. About

yourself, what you want to do. And bring your portfolio. They'll want to see your work."

"Do you think you could come with me? I don't know my way around New York. I've only been there once." She looked terrified. It was hard to believe she was almost four years older than I.

"Don't be scared, you'll do great. Maybe I can come, I'll ask my parents." She gave me a beseeching look as I left.

The whole thing was weird. My father briefed Mary Jane on what she should say, and there we were about a week later, Mary Jane and myself on the train to New York. I was worried all the way down that she was going to get sick, she looked so pale. Neither one of us talked much. We got out at Grand Central and walked to West Fifty-fifth Street, where Mr. Allen had his office. It was a broiling August day. You could feel the heat coming up from the sidewalk so we clung as close to the buildings as we could to keep out of the glare of the sun.

I left Mary Jane at the elevator. "Don't worry," I said. "You'll do great. Lots of luck."

"You'll be here when I come down?" She had a tight hold on her portfolio, and only her face showed how nervous she was. She held herself very straight and looked quite smart in a dark linen dress and black sandals.

"If I'm a few minutes late, just wait. I'm going around to the Museum of Modern Art, and I'll come back in half an hour. Okay?"

"Okay," she said with a weak smile. I gave her a quick hug and watched her get into the elevator.

It took only a few minutes for me to walk to the museum, and I went directly upstairs to the French Impressionists, my favorite school of painting. I wandered around lesiurely looking at the Matisses, the Monets, the Picassos. For a long while I stood in front of a large Renoir, a painting of a mother and her two little girls. They were so serene, so safe-looking in their pretty dresses and with their tranquil faces. Theirs was the kind of life my mother was searching for, I thought, and unexpectedly I felt a strong rapport with the people in the painting and the life it represented. My parents had given me something I believed those little girls had. What could I call it? A sensibility, a discrimination to know the trashy from the good? Suddenly I was glad I had it. Glad, glad. That didn't mean I had to be like my parents, or look down on the popular. But neither did I have to throw away everything they had taught me. At times, I could enjoy both cultures, I knew, because I could *recognize* what was good and bad in both. That was what was important. I could figure out for myself what my taste was, my own lifestyle. As I stood there looking at the Renoir, I felt I was beginning to understand where I stood, as if I had at last chosen to go on a road of my own. Suddenly I became aware a great big world out there, and I was excited about it.

My half hour was up and I hurried back to meet Mary Jane. She didn't come down for about fifteen or twenty minutes, but the minute she stepped out of the elevator I knew things had gone well. Her face had lost its worried look, and she was smiling.

"What happened? Are you going to be accepted?"

"I don't know that yet, but I think maybe I will. He was so nice. Not at all what I expected. He hardly asked me anything. He looked at my drawings and then he kept telling me about the school. As if I needed to be sold on it." She giggled. "He said I'd get a letter. But he asked me about where I'd live and acted like it was all settled."

"Maybe the letter's just a formality. It sounds wonderful. I'm so happy for you."

We were walking along Fifty-fifth Street, and I led her into a coffee shop. "Let's get something to eat."

"I forgot about lunch I'm so excited," she said. "But I'm starving."

After we were seated, Mary Jane looked at me with her face beaming. "I owe it all to you. I don't know how to thank you."

"Don't. Anyway, wait till you get the letter." I was nervous until she had it in writing.

"Did you really go to a museum?" she asked me.

"Yes, sure. Why? You sound surprised."

"I guess because I wouldn't have thought of doing that. I probably would have gone window-shopping."

"If you want to be an artist you should go to museums. Look at paintings."

"I'm going to be a designer, not that kind of an artist."

"That doesn't matter. You might get ideas. Anyway the paintings I looked at are just beautiful." Then I had an idea. "Would you like to go to the museum when we're finished? We have time before our train, and I don't mind going back."

Her face lit up. "You don't? I'd love to."

When we walked into the museum, I was sure Mary Jane had never been in a place like this before. For one thing, she couldn't get over the crowd of people. "All these people here just to look at pictures." She was overwhelmed. "I thought museums are usually empty or have just a few people."

"This place is always jammed," I told her.

I took her to the garden in back to look at the sculpture, and then up to my favorite place. I had only to watch her face as we went from one painting to another to know how much she was enjoying it. She didn't say much but just smiled as she studied each picture. I noted several people glance at her and also smile because of her pleasure. I had to pull her away to catch our train.

Mary Jane was relaxed and less shy on the way home. She talked about her parents, and how much she wanted to get away from the aimless kind of lives they led, the indifference they felt toward her and everyone else. "No one has been as nice to me as Nick, and now you. I couldn't believe my luck when he asked me out, he had everything. I thought he only wanted one thing— you know—but that wasn't it at all. He's sexy enough, God knows, but he cared about me, wanting to help me with my art. I couldn't believe it."

"He's a terrific guy," I agreed.

"He sure is. And you, too."

Listening to Mary Jane talk about Nick and seeing the glow on her face, Matthew came to my mind again. He was someone else whom I had never given a chance. I had been quick to label him dull the same way I had labeled Mary Jane as common. It was scary to think of how much I could go on missing by judging people so quickly and superficially. I hoped then that I would have another chance with Matthew, that somehow I could get to see him again.

Mary Jane's voice broke into my thoughts. "If this comes through, I can really do it. Really be different from my folks, have a different kind of life. Make something of myself."

You sound like me, I said to myself as she stopped talking and became lost in her thoughts. We come from such different worlds, and yet we both want the same thing—to lead our own lives, apart from our parents. This was what I'd been trying to tell my parents: People could be worlds apart on the surface, but you didn't know until you went beneath that how much you might have to share. I was glad I'd found that out.

"Did you have a pleasant time?" my. mother asked me that evening.

"It was one of the nicest days I ever spent."

My mother raised her eyebrows. "Is Mary Jane such good company?"

"We had a good time," was all I said. There were some things I decided that I didn't have to share with anyone, and that day was one of them. The funny thing was, I realized, that I hadn't felt at all badly when Mary Jane had talked about Nick. That must mean something.

As a matter of fact, it meant a lot. After supper I waited until my parents had gone out, and I went to the telephone to call Matthew. It took me a while to dial his number, I was so nervous. There was every chance in the world that he'd give me the cold shoulder.

He was the one who answered the phone and he recognized my voice immediately. I spoke quickly and asked him if he'd like to come over one night for dinner. He actually sounded pleased and said that yes, he'd like that. Then he went on. "I've been dying to go over to Brook Gardens, the amusement park. They've just opened a new roller coaster that's supposed to be terrific. I'm eager to try it, it's supposed to be wild. I love them, don't you? Would you like to go with me?"

I hesitated for only a second. "Sure, that sounds marvelous." We set up a date for the dinner and for the amusement park.

When I hung up the phone I kept sitting by the telephone with a foolish grin on my face. Matthew and a roller coaster. I remembered what Julie had said about kissing and I laughed out loud. It was a wonderful, crazy world and I was going to enjoy every bit of it. I was a lucky girl, I thought, to have so much to choose from.

ABOUT THE AUTHOR

Hila Colman was born and grew up in New York City, where she went to Calhoun School. After graduation, she attended Radcliffe College. Before she started writing for herself, she wrote publicity material and ran a book club. Her first story was sold to the *Saturday Evening Post,* and since then her stories and articles have appeared in many periodicals. Some have been dramatized for television. In 1957, she turned to writing books for teenage girls. One of them, *The Girl From Puerto Rico,* was given a special citation by the Child Study Association of America.

Hila Colman lives in Bridgewater, Connecticut, and has two sons.